2/94

# Too Many
# Crooks
# Spoil the Broth

# Too Many Crooks Spoil the Broth

A Pennsylvania Dutch Mystery with Recipes

## Tamar Myers

A Perfect Crime Book
Doubleday
New York   London   Toronto   Sydney   Auckland

A PERFECT CRIME BOOK
PUBLISHED BY DOUBLEDAY
a division of Bantam Doubleday Dell Publishing Group, Inc.
1540 Broadway, New York, New York 10036

DOUBLEDAY is a trademark of Doubleday,
a division of Bantam Doubleday Dell
Publishing Group, Inc.

*Book design by Anne Ling*

Library of Congress Cataloging-in-Publication-Data

Myers, Tamar.
    Too many crooks spoil the broth : a Pennsylvania Dutch
mystery with recipes / Tamar Myers. — 1st ed.
        p.   cm.
    "A Perfect crime book."
    1. Women detectives—Pennsylvania—Fiction.   2.
Hotelkeepers—Pennsylvania—Fiction.   3. Mennonites—
Pennsylvania—Fiction.
    I. Title.
PS3563.Y475T66   1994
813'.54—dc20                                    93-13424
                                                    CIP


ISBN 0-385-47139-4

Printed in the United States of America

January 1994

1   3   5   7   9   10   8   6   4   2

FIRST EDITION

*To my loving husband, Jeff*

# ACKNOWLEDGMENTS

To all those people who encouraged and supported my efforts, thank you.

With special thanks to my friend Yael, who told me I could; to Marcie Banks, who told me I should; and to Nancy Yost, my agent, who told me I would.

I also acknowledge and appreciate the efforts of my editor, Judy Kern.

Under duress, I will acknowledge my children, whose interruptions were aggravating, but not fatal. Not to mention my two cats, whose frequent trips across the keyboard made life interesting.

And of course, ultimately I owe it all to my parents. Thanks, Mother, for your Amish heritage. And yes, Dad, the book *will* be published!

# Too Many
# Crooks
# Spoil the Broth

# Chapter One

I knew at once that the screamer was Susannah. Hers is an exceptionally high-pitched scream, and while it won't break any glasses, it will curdle milk and put the hens off laying.

When I got there, Susannah was still standing just inside the bedroom door, but she had stopped screaming. Her mouth, however, continued to open and close with the regularity of a pump valve. Come to think of it, she could still have been screaming, but somewhere out of my decibel range.

I could see at once what the problem was. Sprawled across the sleigh bed, half-draped in Mama's best Dresden Plate quilt, was a corpse. A corpse, as opposed to a body. There is a difference, you know.

In my forty-three years I've seen a few dead bodies, but this was my first corpse. The bodies had all belonged to people who knew they were going to die, or who were at peace with themselves when their time came. Seeing them was hard enough.

A corpse is different because the remains belong to someone who has died in mental as well as physical agony. This is my own definition, of course, but I'm sure you'll agree.

Even from a distance it was clear that this was a corpse. These were not the vacantly staring eyes that one traditionally associates with death. The eyes of this corpse seemed to be focused in rage at the ceiling, although a quick glance in that direction revealed nothing more than a few wispy cobwebs Susannah's broom had missed.

The corpse's open mouth was a dead giveaway too. I know, most people die with their mouths open, but the lips on this one were pulled back, and there was something about their position that made me think their owner had died cursing. Perhaps those lips were still issuing silent curses, like Susannah's silent screams.

And take the hands. People usually die with their hands open too. I mean, when they die their muscles relax and they let go of whatever they've been holding. Not so with this corpse. This corpse was clutching Mama's Dresden Plate quilt so tightly, I was afraid we'd have to do some cutting to part corpse from quilt. Cutting fingers, I mean, not the quilt.

Not that the quilt was in such good shape anyway. Both my eyes and my nose told me there was at least one part of the corpse that had relaxed.

"Gosh darn!" I said. I swear, that is as bad as I can curse.

Susannah began to make some noises that were neither speech nor screams.

"Get a grip on it," I admonished her. "I'll call the police, but in the meantime, you run downstairs and see if we have any borax in the laundry room. If not, dash out and get some. If this quilt's been ruined, someone's going to pay!"

I know that might sound a little callous to you, but you

have to stand tough if you expect to succeed in the business world. And I, for one, was succeeding remarkably well, all things considered.

We'd been farmers, you see. Mennonite farmers in the Allegheny Mountains of southern Pennsylvania. Ours was primarily a dairy farm, which Papa ran with the help of a kinsman, Mose Hostetler. Mama and Freni, Mose's wife, did the gardening and took care of the chickens. Some years Mama made more selling eggs than Papa did selling milk.

I'm sure I'd only confuse you if I said that Mose and Freni were third cousins, and that both of them were somehow related to Papa, and Freni was related to Mama as well. I suppose it would confuse you even more if I mentioned that Mose and Freni weren't even Mennonites, but Church Amish. Suffice it to say, the Hostetlers were family, as well as employees.

The routine of our farm, the love of our family, and the firm foundation of our church made me think that I would live my entire life feeling absolutely secure, if not a little bored. Then one day something tragic happened that turned my life upside down.

Papa and Mama were on their way west to Somerset when their car was rear-ended in the Allegheny Tunnel. The vehicle that did this was a semitrailer loaded to the gills with state-of-the-art running shoes. The driver of the truck was loaded to the gills with Mogen David 20/20. The authorities believe my parents might have survived this accident, had there been no one in front of them. Unfortunately, there was another truck in front of them, this one a shiny, silver tanker. Mama and Papa died needlessly in a mishmash of sneakers and pasteurized milk.

That was ten years ago, when I was thirty-three and my sister, Susannah, twenty-three. Fortunately for us, the farm had been paid for a generation earlier, but still we had all those cows and chickens to contend with. The Hostetlers were, after all, nearing retirement age, and we couldn't stick them with all the work. Perhaps the four of us might have been able to make a go of it, but Susannah, who never was much of a worker anyway, ran off and married a Presbyterian —something she never would have done had Mama and Papa been alive!

Then one day I picked up a magazine that had an article about bed-and-breakfast establishments, and cerebral lightning struck. Why not, I pondered, go two steps further and offer lunch and dinner as well? So, to make a long story short, that's how the PennDutch Inn was begun.

In retrospect, I am amazed at how quickly the pieces fell into place. Sure, Freni Hostetler was opposed to the idea, but she's just generally allergic to change. Mose, on the other hand, thought it was a great idea. Normally the Amish, even the more liberal ones like Mose and Freni, don't like mixing with outsiders, but Mose liked the idea of milking all those cows by himself even less. In no time at all, we sold off all the cows but two, got the chickens down to a more manageable flock, and built an addition to the farmhouse.

With the exception of remodeling the kitchen to meet health codes and updating the plumbing, there was very little work needed on the existing house. I didn't even bother to redecorate. All of Mama's furnishings had been in the family for years, some for generations, and while they looked old and commonplace to me, to the outside world they were antiques. Even Mama's hobby, quilt-making, finally paid off, because

there were enough quilts by then to put one on each guest
bed.

And while I don't really believe in luck, it was with me
nonetheless. I had advertised in both Pittsburgh and Philadelphia papers, and among my first guests was a yuppie reviewer
who fancied herself a connoisseur of Americana, and of the
Pennsylvania Dutch in particular. Never mind that she
thought our plain posture was all an act, and that Freni's blue
broadcloth dresses and white net prayer bonnet were nothing
more than a costume. What matters is that she gave us a rave
review, and started a stampede of well-heeled, highfalutin cus-
tomers who have kept right on coming. I have not advertised
again.

Of course I did the sensible thing and jacked up the prices.
Connoisseurs are only happy when paying a premium. Since
that first, and fateful, review, I have jacked up my rates six
times, and my waiting list keeps getting longer.

Another thing I did was to institute the old work ethic.
On the parlor wall I hung a sampler with a verse from 1
Corinthians: "We work hard with our own hands." That the
verse is taken out of context does not matter—yuppies are not
all that familiar with the Bible. The point is, my guests are
expected to clean their own rooms every day, and even to help
out with the common rooms. This doesn't seem to bother
them one whit, as long as they remain convinced that this is
part of our culture. Most of them do. For those few who don't
want to immerse themselves so thoroughly in the Amish-
Mennonite heritage, Susannah and I are glad to take over. For
an extra fee, of course. You'd be surprised how much people
will pay for abuse, provided they can view it as a cultural
experience.

At any rate, what with our low operating expenses and our astonishingly high income, we managed to pay off the new wing in no time at all, and start squirreling some of those greenbacks away. My goal is to someday travel to all those interesting places our guests hail from. In fact, I'd like to see the whole world, every bit of it—except those parts that are permanently covered by ice and snow.

But for now, at least until I can find a replacement more competent than Susannah (who divorced her Presbyterian and moved back home), I have to content myself with seeing the world through books, and the eyes of our guests. Since Mama and Papa's tragic accident, my perspective has changed drastically. But then, when your world turns upside down, your perspective can't help but change.

So you can see now, can't you, why the corpse on the old sleigh bed was upsetting, but not quite as upsetting as the fact that it had soiled Mama's Dresden Plate quilt? Of course, it was probably all my fault to begin with. I had gotten too busy, and didn't take my usual care in selecting the guests that first weekend of deer-hunting season. What follows is exactly what happened.

# Chapter Two

They began to arrive on Sunday afternoon, the Sunday following Thanksgiving. Deer-hunting season was to begin at dawn the following day. Normally I try to pick deer hunters as my guests at that time, even though I am personally repulsed by the idea of shooting anything that isn't trying to mug you. My reason for welcoming hunters is very Biblical. Didn't the prophet Ezekiel say something about there being a time and season for everything? Although the PennDutch Inn is at least six miles from State Game Land No. 48, every year our land gets overrun by hunters. I figure that if any of my patrons must risk an accidental bullet, it may as well be hunters.

I was particularly pleased with the lot I'd selected this year (you wouldn't believe how long my waiting list is, and don't think for a minute that it is first come, first served). Four of the week's guests were to be women. Women hunters, imagine that! Not that women can't be hunters too, it's just this was the first time a woman had stated on her application that she

was a hunter. Well, with the exception of one woman, who it
turned out was really a hunting groupie in search of two-
legged bucks carrying a lot of greenbacks. But that happened a
long time ago, and is another story.

Anyway, I had just gotten home from church, and hadn't
even had time to fix myself a bite of lunch, when the first of
these four women showed up unexpectedly. Check-in time is
three p.m., and it was only a couple of minutes past noon
when this creature appeared at the front door, so can you
blame me for being at least a little miffed?

And another thing, I hate being startled. People who
sneak up behind you, even if it is not their intention to scare
you, deserve a special place in hell. I know that's a terrible
thing to think, especially on a Sunday, but ever since I was a
child, and my cousin Sam sneaked up behind me and suddenly
dangled a live blacksnake in my face, causing me to lose control of my bladder, I've harbored a shameful hatred of sneaky
people. Of course Susannah knows this and torments me with
her knowledge. One night, just a year ago, I opened the door
to my bedroom closet, only to find Susannah in there, behind
my dresses, with her chin resting on the hanger bar, and the
light of a flashlight shining up onto her face. She had her
mouth open in a snarl, and was wearing those silly plastic
teeth kids stick in their mouths on Halloween. Of course I
screamed, and maybe dampened my bloomers just a little.
Meanwhile Susannah howled with laughter. And this from a
woman who will never see the sunny side of thirty again?

But back to the woman at the front door. If she had rung
the bell, knocked, or even walked in loudly, I wouldn't have
minded so much. But she just stood there, outside, like a giant
moth pressed up against the screen of the front door. She even

looked like a moth. Everything about her was a grayish beige. Light ash brown, I think they call it. I call it mousy. If she'd been a larger woman, she could have gotten a job as a used sofa in the bargain basement of the Salvation Army store, or had she at least worn a large green hat, she might well have passed for a tree. You get the picture.

"What is it you want?" I said perhaps a little too sharply.

The giant moth did not flutter away. "I've come to register in your inn."

I was taken aback. Normally I put on a little show for my guests. Atmosphere is, after all, what most of them have come seeking. Obviously it was now too late to trot out the accent, or to put on plainer-looking duds. "Aren't you just a wee bit early, Miss?" I asked as pleasantly as I could. "I mean, check-in isn't for another three hours."

The mousy moth opened her medium-sized mitt and revealed a folded fifty-dollar bill. "For your extra trouble," she said in her nondescript voice.

"Come on in, dear," I cried warmly. "Here, let me help you with your luggage."

But there was only one, tan, medium-sized suitcase, and the woman insisted on handling it herself.

"Name, please?" I asked when we were at the desk.

"Heather Brown."

"That figures."

"Pardon me?"

I had to lie slightly to cover for my rudeness. The Lord, I'm sure, understands that kind of thing. Maybe two wrongs don't make a right, but sometimes that's all there is left. "What I mean is, you were the first of this week's guests to make your reservation, and now you're the first to check in. The early bird catches the worm, like they say, and you've just caught yourself one of the larger rooms in the new wing."

Instead of being pleased, Miss Brown looked more like I'd given her a real worm. "This is *the* PennDutch Inn, isn't it? In Hernia, Pennsylvania?"

"None other," I said with justifiable pride.

"And I was the very first one to make reservations for the coming week?" Due to the Inn's immense popularity amongst well-heeled culture seekers, especially on the East Coast, I insist that all guests pay up front for a minimum of one week. It saves on washing sheets.

Miss Brown began to fumble for something in her camel-colored purse. "Why, then I'm very surprised. I mean, I only made the request a few weeks ago, and I've heard that your inn is very popular, especially with the 'in crowd.' " She laughed, the innocuous sort of chuckle one hears on TV laugh tracks.

"Of course it is," I assured her.

"I've even heard that movie stars sometimes stay here."

"Barbra Streisand was very nice," I said modestly.

"And of course, since you're only hours away from D.C., I suppose you see a fair number of those folks as well?"

"You bet your bippy! As a matter of fact, Congressman Ream and his wife are expected today." Honestly, I didn't mean to let that kind of information slip out. Normally, I'm as tight-lipped as a pickle sucker when it comes to my current guests. But there was something about Miss Brown, maybe it was her very blandness, that made me want to impress her.

How do you tell when a moth is impressed? Miss Brown said, "Gee, that's exciting," but she sounded as about as excited as Susannah does when I ask her to help me fold laundry.

I dislike people who speak in monotones almost as much as I dislike people who sneak up on you.

"Do you want the Amish Lifestyle Plan Option?" I asked pleasantly, nonetheless.

Miss Brown had finished fumbling in her camel-colored purse and was displaying a wad of bills big enough to choke a hog fresh off a two-day fast. "For my bill," she said. "And what I really would like is to be left alone."

"Sure thing, Miss Brown." After all, she wasn't being nasty, and I've yet to hear a boom box that can put out anywhere near as many decibels as do-re-me.

"Now, where do you want me parking my car?"

"Just leave it where it is for now and I'll park it," I said. To be too proud to take tips is a sin in itself.

I showed Miss Brown to her room, after a brief tug of war over her tan suitcase, which she, I regret to say, won. Unlike most guests, Miss Brown seemed oblivious to the quaint surroundings. Even the impossibly steep stairs that lead up to the second floor didn't seem to perturb her. It was obvious that she hadn't come for the ambience, yet I didn't see hide nor hair of any sort of hunting equipment.

"Would you like me to bring in your guns when I move the car?" I asked.

For the first time I saw emotion—perhaps amusement— flicker across her face. "I haven't any guns."

"But on your application you stated that you were a hunter." Mennonites are not big on hunting, but if someone was going to do it, I would just as soon it was a woman. A woman hunter, in my opinion, would simply shoot her deer and then go home. No need for male bonding and the ritual downing of six-packs. For some men, on the other hand, bagging a buck has developed into a week-long religious experience that follows its own complicated liturgy. Surely only someone possessing male gonads could possibly hope to understand what really goes on. For example, several years ago I foolishly allowed Susannah to put a ceramic deer out on the lawn as an ornament. The first day of deer season it got shattered to smithereens. And Susannah had painted it pink!

Anyway I was disappointed when Miss Brown informed me that she had never hunted deer, and never intended to do so. She was a photo-hunter, she said, and her bag was filled with expensive photographic equipment. She had come to shoot pictures of the hunters shooting the deer. She was a photographic essayist for some magazine that had "Illustrated" in the title. Did I want to see her credentials, or perhaps even read one of her articles?

I did not. Because of the PennDutch's enormous success amongst the moneyed crowd, I had become quite inured to famous people, and I certainly didn't count bland little Miss Brown as a celebrity. Now if Paul Theroux wanted to show me his latest manuscript, that was something else.

"And I won't be taking my meals here," said Miss Brown. "Remember, I said that on my application?"

I did remember then, and with gratitude. Miss Brown probably ate like a moth, and whatever it is that moths eat, I'm sure Freni doesn't cook it. I made a mental note to examine the bed linens for holes before Miss Brown checked out.

I cheerfully parked her car for her, and, as expected, received a nice fat tip. Miss Brown's car, incidentally, was about as flashy as her person. It was certainly not a status car for a crack reporter. Frankly, it was as ugly as sin, even one of Susannah's sins. I don't know about car makes, but this one was asphalt gray, with mud-brown seats. Surely driving a car like that on a foggy day would be a risk taken only by bungee-jumpers. Even though I'd parked the car myself, on my way back to the house I looked over my shoulder twice just to make sure it was really there.

With Miss Brown tucked quietly away in her room, I ate a quick sandwich, and then settled down for my favorite Sunday afternoon activity—napping. If I time it right, and things work out the way they are supposed to, I can get a good two-hour nap in between church and the arrival of my first guests. Of course I don't really sleep the whole two hours; that would be far too decadent, even on a Sunday. Normally I just sit back in my favorite rocker, and alternately doze, read a book, and worry about Susannah. This Sunday, however, thanks to the early arrival of Miss Brown, my schedule was thrown off, and the sudden commotion at the front door caught me in mid-doze.

I could tell instantly that the two women who lurched through the outside porch door at precisely three p.m., each carrying one large and one small suitcase, were not hunters either. Or even groupies. These women had never been outdoors longer than the time it takes to get from the mall to an outlying parking spot.

I immediately vacated my favorite rocker and ambled to my welcoming position behind the front desk. My office is merely the front left corner of the main sitting room, which is the first room you enter off the front porch. In the old days this was the dining room, where our large, extended family would congregate regularly for meals.

Mama wouldn't recognize it now. Gone is the massive oak

table that it took four men to lift. In its place is a large oval braided rug that took Freni and me six months to make. The furniture, which now rings the walls, is a hodgepodge of old rockers and hard, high-backed chairs. Only one of them is comfortable, and I grab it whenever I get a chance. Mixed in with the chairs are the occasional spinning wheel, butter churn, and the like. Securely fastened to the walls, so that no one need worry, are such things as washboards, horse harnesses, and even a two-man tree saw. Usually people gasp when they first see this room and mutter complimentary phrases that include the words "quaint" and "homey."

The two women staggered in from the porch, and, like Miss Brown, seemed oblivious to their surroundings. But it didn't take a genius to figure out that they'd been arguing.

"Goot aftahnoon," I said from behind the counter. I'm always careful not to sound too friendly, because when people pay a lot of money they expect at least a little condescension. Why else do you think Paris is so popular?

"We're the Parker party," said the older of the two women. "I'm Ms. Jeanette Parker, and this is my friend, Linda McMahon."

"Velcommen to zee PennDeutsch," I said. "I'm Magdalena Yoder, proprietress." Now don't get me wrong. I hate talking in a fake German accent, and as for being a "proprietress," doesn't that sound like the night job some women take when they move to the big city? But, my guests seem to love it.

Ms. Parker was not impressed. "You should have our reservations. For two rooms. In the new wing."

Her companion began to shift her weight from one foot to the other, and her face reddened considerably. "I—uh—I think I only booked one room for us, Jeanette."

"You what?"

"They are supposed to be very large rooms. Aren't they, Mrs. Yoder?" She looked beseechingly at me for confirmation.

"It's 'Miss.' " I dropped the accent. It's too hard to maintain in the midst of conflict, and I could smell conflict coming as surely as I can smell Freni cooking sauerkraut on a hot summer day.

"What?" demanded the older woman. She was in her mid-forties, and seemed to be very self-assured. For some reason red hair intimidates me, and this woman's carrot-orange do was no exception.

I swallowed a couple of times. "It's 'Miss,' not 'Mrs.' I've never been married." Susannah delights in reminding me of this.

Ms. Parker's blue eyes stared coldly at me through her pale red lashes. It was the kind of stare teachers give you just before they accuse you of being a smart aleck. "I'm not interested in your marital status. Do you by chance have an extra room?"

"But, Jeanette, I already checked when I sent in the application. She doesn't have any other rooms." The younger woman, perhaps only in her early twenties, was still blushing. Frankly, the emotionally induced infusion of red was an improvement over her otherwise anemic appearance.

"Is that true? Are you all out of rooms?"

"Technically," I said.

"Technically? What's that supposed to mean?"

"Well, I could give you my sister's room, I suppose. It's in the new wing. But it is an imposition."

"Would double the rate make it less of an imposition?"

"It's no trouble at all," I said, and then smiled sweetly.

Actually it was going to be more trouble than it was worth.

Ever since her divorce, Susannah had taken up residence in one of the three bedrooms in the new wing. These are the largest, most comfortable rooms in the Inn, and of course the most expensive. The reason I had not put up a fight was because the only sensible alternative was to have Susannah move in with me.

Before I give you the impression that I'm a whiner, let me explain about Susannah. She is, without doubt, the messiest adult in the world. Susannah would be an inspiration to any teenager. And in addition to the mess, and the fact that Susannah keeps immorally late hours, there is the matter of her dog. If only it were a real dog, like a shepherd or a collie. But Susannah's dog is one of those rat-sized things that yips constantly in a high-pitched voice when it's not nipping at your ankles. I'll even confess that I've been tempted, on more than one occasion, to aid the dog in some mysterious disappearing act, but alas, Susannah is never more than five feet away.

"Linda, pay her for the room so we can get settled," Ms. Parker ordered.

"Well, you do realize," I said quickly, "that it will take a few minutes before housekeeping can get around to cleaning the extra room?"

"She can wait in my room," Ms. Parker said irritably. I thought I saw the hint of a smile play across Linda's kind, but rather plain face. "Linda, pay her, and let's get a move on."

Linda scurried to obey, proffering me both her Visa and Mastercard. I selected one of the cards and took down the number. "Would you be wanting the Amish Lifestyle Plan Option with this room?"

"Pardon me?"

"We don't clean motel rooms," said Ms. Jeanette Parker curtly.

I noted that by upping the price. "Three meals a day?"

She brusquely nodded her affirmation. "I'm a vegan, Linda's a lacto."

"I think I'm a Virgo," I said, trying to cooperate.

"She means we're vegetarians," said Linda quickly. "I eat dairy products, but no eggs or fish. Jeanette eats only fruits and vegetables. And of course grains."

I tried to smile, but I knew Freni would throw a fit. She does all the cooking for the PennDutch, and it's done her way. Meals are served family style, and the choices are between starch and grease. "I'll see what we can do."

"What do you mean by 'I'll see'? Linda, you did mark that down on the application, didn't you?"

Linda chewed nervously on a nail. "I'm pretty sure."

I was pretty sure she hadn't, but just to prove them wrong, I dug their application out of my files and spread it on the counter.

"There! See?" said Ms. Parker triumphantly.

I studied the sheet. Sure enough the words "lacto" and "vegan" did appear, after their names. But you can hardly fault me for not recognizing their significance, can you? At least a third of my applicants have letters after their names, but until now I'd always assumed they stood for titles or degrees. "I'll speak to the cook," I said humbly.

"Very well," said Ms. Parker magnanimously. "Please have the bellboy bring our bags up at once."

We have no bellboy. The only male in our operation is Mose, and I wasn't about to saddle a seventy-three-year-old

man with suitcases that two healthy women could carry themselves. "Carrying your own bags is part of the Amish Lifestyle
Plan Option," I said matter-of-factly. "Bellboys cost extra."

"Put it on the bill."

I did. Then I went around the counter and picked up the
two closest bags, tucking the smaller one under my arm. Then
I got the remaining two. Slowly I straightened. "Follow me."

"We can't let her carry all of them," I heard Linda whisper
to her companion. "She's too old!"

I straightened my back even more and led the way briskly
down the back hall and up our unfortunately steep stairs.
There is nothing quite like a jolt of adrenaline to rejuvenate
this middle-aged body, and the Mss. McMahon and Parker
were keeping me well supplied with energy.


Just as I thought, cousin Freni almost blew a gasket when I
told her she had two vegetarians to cook for that evening.
Freni's temper functions just like a pressure cooker. The steam
builds up slowly but steadily and, if unchecked, is liable to
explode with dire consequences.

"I'm making chicken and dumplings and they can eat it or
not."

"Chicken and dumplings is fine for the rest of us," I said
soothingly. "But we need to think up some vegetable dishes
for those two."

"There's carrots, onions, and celery in the chicken stock.
If you like, I'll throw in a potato or two, even though that's
not the right way to make dumplings. And there's pickled
beets and eggs on the side."

I smiled encouragingly, despite the fact that I have been

trying for years to convince Freni that eggs are not a vegetable. "That's the spirit, Freni, but I'm afraid they're going to want their vegetables cooked outside of the chicken broth."

"Fine." But of course it wasn't. I could tell by the way the lines around Freni's mouth were beginning to disappear that the pressure was building. Foolishly I pressed just a little further. Trapped between Freni and Ms. Parker was not a comfortable place to be, but at least I knew what Freni's limitations were.

"What about fruit, Freni? Are we serving any fruit?"

"There's apple butter with the bread, and apple pie with cheese for dessert."

I'd long since given up trying to convince Freni that cheese was not a fruit. To Freni the hard-to-classify foods (for Freni that included eggs, grains, and dairy products) took on the category of the food with which they were commonly served. By logical extension, macaroni and cheese would be a fruit dish, something with which Freni would have no quarrel.

"And there's cream for the coffee!" added Freni triumphantly.

"How about serving some stewed fruit? Maybe a nice compote that you put away in September?"

Freni's lines began to disappear faster, and I knew I'd gone about as far as I dared. "Anything else, Magdalena?"

I was about to say "no," when I remembered Ms. Parker's cold blue eyes staring at me through their pale red lashes. "I don't suppose any of that compote was put up without sugar?" I began to back out of the kitchen. "And could you bake up a batch of oat or whole grain bread?" I almost sprinted to the sitting room.

. . .

I had just gotten settled back down in my rocker when the next guest arrived. He was a very tall, skinny man, with an eggshell complexion, who was dressed from head to toe in blue denim. Even his shoes were denim. Although he looked frail, he almost beat me to the front desk. He was not carrying any suitcases, only a small backpack.

"Goot aftahnoon. Velcommen to zee PennDeutsch Inn."

"Raidstu Yiddish?"

I put a lid on the fake accent and opened the register. "You are Mr.—?"

"Teitlebaum. Joel Teitlebaum. Ova."

"Magdalena Yoder. Mercury Comet."

"I mean that I eat eggs. But no fish or dairy products, of course."

"Of course. Meat?"

Joel Teitlebaum blanched and may even have swayed a little. "Of course not!"

I nodded. At least I had figured out on my own that we had another vegetarian on our hands. "Would you like the Amish Lifestyle Package Option?" I asked bravely. These were not the kinds of guests I was used to.

"Yes, I would."

I smiled in relief. "You'll find the broom, dustpan, and dust cloth in your room closet. So are the bathroom supplies. Rooms must be cleaned and beds made before breakfast. You do want three meals a day, don't you?"

"Are your eggs organic?"

I nodded assuringly, which isn't the same as lying. As far as I know, the only inorganic eggs are the marble kind sold in gift shops. "Yours is room three, in this wing, on the second floor."

When I got back from showing Joel his room, I found a party of three waiting for me at the desk. "Goot aftahnoon!" I called cheerily. Believe me, forced cheer is an art that can be learned, no matter how grumpy it makes you.

I knew at once that this party consisted of United States Congressman Garrett Ream, his wife, the socialite Lydia Johns Ream, and the Congressman's aide, somebody James. I knew this not only because they were to be our only party of three that week, but also because I had seen both Reams' pictures in the paper dozens of times.

Garrett Ream had only one more year left until reelection, and everyone knew that his next step was going to be the Senate. It was also a sure bet that the United States Senate was only a stepping stone to the White House. Tall, dark, and handsome, with an I.Q. higher than room temperature, Garrett Ream seemingly had everything going for him. Especially his wife.

Lydia Johns Ream was none other than the daughter of Senator Archibald Johns and heiress Margaret Lyons Needmore. It had been said from her cradle days on, that whomever Lydia married would someday be President of the United States. The hand that rocked Lydia's cradle was surely employed by the parents of a future First Lady.

"Velcommen to zee PennDeutsch Inn." I even bowed slightly.

"Can it, fraulein," said Congressman Ream. "Send someone to get the bags. Is the manager in?"

I must admit, my mouth had fallen open wide enough to stuff in even one of Freni's dumplings, but that was no excuse for what he said next. "Speakatee zee English?"

"Apparently about as well as you," I couldn't resist saying. I was still in a state of shock. This man was an elected public official, and even though I didn't live in his district, it was pretty darn cheeky of him to be so rude. Next year, when he ran for the Senate, we'd see who got the last laugh.

"Well, if you speak English, Miss, then hop to it and get the manager and bellboy out here, pronto!"

I glared at him, pretending I was Ms. Parker and he was me. "I am the manager, mis-ter!"

"You?"

"Darling," said his wife, stepping forward and taking his left arm in both of hers, "let's just check in, shall we? It's been a long drive."

I could tell just by the way she spoke that the lady had class. Everything about her whispered (a soft, cultured whisper, of course) class. The way she moved was pure class. From the tip of her expensively but elegantly coiffed hair to the tips of her make-Imelda-Marcos-envious shoes, she looked classy. What then was she doing with such a clod? Besides the fact that he was handsome?

"I can take care of this, dear," the clod muttered under his breath.

The class act didn't seem to hear him. "We're Congressman and Mrs. Ream," she said smoothly, "and this is Mr. James, my husband's aide. I believe you have us down for reservations."

I pretended to scan the register. "Ah yes, Mrs. Ream. I have you down right here. Are you vegans, lactos, or ovas?"

"We're Episcopalians." A slight smile played at the corners of her perfectly made-up mouth.

"I see. Will that be the Amish Lifestyle Package Option, or do you want Housekeeping snooping in your rooms?"

Again the slight smile. "Why, I think it would be fun to rough it for a change. Put us all down for A.L.P.O." I must mention here that the Ream party had booked three rooms. Couples of their status might occasionally conjugate, but they never cohabit.

"The three-meal plan?"

"By all means. I'm looking forward to your famous Amish cooking." Bingo! A woman after my own heart, and one that might even bring a smile to Freni's lips.

"Very well, Mrs. Ream. Oh, there is one thing. In addition to being the manager and owner, I might add I'm also the bellboy. Now, I would be happy to bring all your bags in myself, except that—"

"No need to say more. Please Delbert, be a darling and get the bags." She had half-turned to Delbert James, who had been standing impassively in the background. She turned back to me. "This is a very charming place you have here, Mrs.—?"

"Yoder. It's Miss Yoder. Magdalena Yoder. Thank you."

"Not at all. Perhaps when you have a moment you can tell me all about life here in Hershey, Pennsylvania."

"That's Hernia." I stole a glance at the Congressman, who, as it happened, was glowering at me from his safe position slightly to the rear of his wife.

"I beg your pardon?"

"Hershey's the chocolate town. The PennDutch is located in Hernia, Pennsylvania."

Lydia Ream laughed then. Actually it was more of a

chuckle, but people of her class don't chuckle, do they? "I would love to hear all about Hernia, then."

At that moment the impassive but not bad-looking Delbert James came back in with the first load of luggage. Reluctantly, I gathered up the three necessary keys and led the way through the back hallway and up the unfortunately steep stairs. Mrs. Ream followed directly behind me, and the whole way I was acutely conscious of that fact that I am not a size six with toddler-sized shoes who could move with the grace of a ballerina. So, my ancestors were peasants, can I help it?

And wouldn't you know, this time I didn't even make it all the way back to the sitting room before the next and final guest of the day arrived. Would that I had!

# Chapter Three

I got back to the sitting room to find Susannah and a man engaged in animated conversation by the check-in counter. Immediately my blood began to boil. Fortunately I am not like Freni, who takes a long time to build up steam and then explodes, sometimes with dire consequences. I'm constantly exploding—little tiny puffs, which, like flatulence, are temporarily noxious but ultimately harmless.

When it comes to Susannah, the puffs may be louder, but there is always justification. Susannah, I'm sorry to say, is a slovenly, slothful slut. I know, that's a terrible thing to say about one's own sister, and both Mama and Papa would roll over in their graves if they heard me, but it's the plain truth.

It was bad enough when Susannah married the Presbyterian, but when she divorced him and began sleeping with other men, she became a full-fledged adulteress in the eyes of my church and just about everybody living in the environs of

Hernia, Pennsylvania. Susannah is the first person ever in my entire family history, which can be traced back to sixteenth-century Swiss roots, to get a divorce. Believe me, I'm not judging her. If she had to get a divorce, then she had to. But what she should have done afterward was to withdraw from the public view and buckle down to work here at the Inn. Not Susannah!

Susannah is constantly running around, not only in Hernia, but as far away as Somerset and Bedford. She chews gum like a cow munching alfalfa. She wears makeup, perms her hair, and even paints her nails! In the summertime she frequently wears sleeveless dresses, and once I actually caught her wearing shorts. And of course you know where these ideas come from—TV! Susannah keeps a portable TV in her room, even though I won't allow her to put up an antenna.

Please don't get me wrong. There's nothing immoral about wanting to get out into the world. As you already know, I myself want to travel some day. It is, however, possible to deport oneself modestly and with decorum. And of course, one must never, ever sleep with a man outside the bounds of matrimony. And I'm not just talking about the risk of getting AIDS here, I'm talking about sin, something Susannah admits she finds delightful!

I might even be able to deal with a sinful, sexy Susannah, but add to that slothfulness and slobbiness, and it's just too much to bear. Susannah will never willingly lift a finger, unless it's to paint another finger. So I get stuck doing ninety percent of the work around the PennDutch, Mose and Freni excluded. What little I can badger Susannah into doing, usually has to be redone by me anyway, so what's the point?

Thank the Lord that Papa and Mama, in their earthly wisdom, left the controlling interest in the farm to me. Perhaps they had been given a divine premonition of the impending Presbyterian. At any rate, if it weren't for my tight rein on things, both of us would be out on the street, and at least one of us making her living from it.

So you can see how my blood began to boil when I saw my sister, who was just now coming home from the night before, in the sitting room, talking to a disreputable-looking character.

"Get behind me, Satan," I said loud enough for Susannah to hear. The temptation to strangle was almost unbearable.

Susannah laughed and foolishly tried to hide a half-smoked cigarette by sticking it in her purse. "This, Billy," she said by way of introduction, "is my older sister, Magdalena. But you can call her Mags. Everyone does."

Although disreputable-looking, the character she'd dragged home exhibited more manners than she did. "Pleased to meet you, ma'am," he said.

"It's Miss Yoder," I said pointedly.

"Billy Dee Grizzle, ma'am."

"Mr. Grizzle," I acknowledged his politeness. Even as I was saying his name, I knew it sounded familiar, and I knew why. William D. Grizzle was the last name still unchecked on today's page of the register. "You're not," I asked sheepishly, "a friend of Susannah's?" Perhaps I emphasized the word "friend" just a bit too much.

Billy Dee smiled broadly and displayed a set of remarkably white teeth. Remarkable in that Billy Dee looked like the kind of man who would chew tobacco. "Miss Susannah and I have

just become acquainted, ma'am. She's a very friendly young
woman, but we ain't friends yet."

There was something about the way Billy Dee said the
word "young" that made me feel flushed. It was as if Billy Dee
had meant to say he couldn't be bothered by someone as
young as Susannah.

Susannah must have noticed it too. "I'll leave you two
old folks alone to chaw down on history," she said. She
might have meant to be cute, but it just sounded rude to
me.

"Bye, ma'am. Nice meeting you," said Billy Dee sin-
cerely.

"Not so fast," I said to Susannah. "There's something you
ought to know."

"Mags, I only want a hot shower before I hit the hay.
Can you tape-record the lecture so I can play it back
later?"

I tried not to let my irritation show. "You better shower
and hit the hay in my room. Room 5 has been rented."

Susannah said a word that I refuse to repeat, and started
toward the back, but I stopped her. "You need to clear your
things out of Room 5 first. And give it a quick going over." I
was being kind. I should have told her to bulldoze the room
and then torch it.

Susannah started to protest, but her whining was eclipsed
by the sounds emanating from her purse.

"What in the world is that?" I asked.

"Oh, Shnookums," she wailed, "Mommy is so sorry!" Apparently there wasn't room in her pocketbook for both her
still-lit cigarette and that bizarre excuse for a dog I told you

about. Susannah fled in search of water, leaving a faint trail of smoke.

I smiled bravely at Billy Dee. "Good help is hard to find these days."

He laughed, a good knee-slapping laugh. "I think I'm gonna enjoy my stay here, Miss Yoder."

I hope I didn't blush. "Magdalena, if you like. But let's get down to business, shall we? First of all, vegan, lacto, or ova?"

"Carne."

"I beg your pardon?"

"Meat-eater." He thumped his chest. "That's me. Good old-fashioned consumer of flesh. But I see the others have all checked in."

"The others? You know them?"

"Let's see. A tall, skinny dude, late twenties, eyes like a deer. Nice-enough guy, though."

"That'd be Mr. Teitlebaum."

"Yeah, the Jew from Philadelphia. Now the other two. One's young, kinda mousy. The other, well, how does anyone describe Big Red kindly?"

"That's them," I agreed enthusiastically, but I refrained from mentioning their names. I had overstepped my bounds by identifying Joel Teitlebaum. My job is to check people in and out, not to play twenty questions with my guests. "You know these people?"

"We're all A.P.E.S."

"What was that?"

"We're all card-carrying members of the Animal Parity Endowment Society."

"I tend to vote Republican myself." That's not really true. I vote all over the board, but it seemed like the right thing to say to even the score.

He chuckled. "What I mean is that we all belong to an organization that concerns itself with the rights of animals."

"What kind of animals?" Dogs like Susannah's have no rights.

"Well," he drawled, "in this case, deer."

I undoubtedly stared at him. I was in shock. Finally, after a few tries, I found my voice. "You're kidding! You mean you're not here to hunt deer?" I fumbled around in my files. Sure enough, Billy Dee and all the others he'd just mentioned had stated on their applications that they wanted to be here for the opening of deer season. "But it says—"

"Does it say why we want to be here?"

"You've got to be kidding," I said again. I was in no mood for jokes, but this had better be one just the same.

His face now lacked joviality, which made him look even more like a redneck, although he was acting less like one. "No, ma'am, I'm deadly serious. We're here to stop the deer hunt."

I was having trouble believing what I was hearing. "Whose deer hunt? Those are state game lands out there. Tomorrow morning they'll be swarming with hunters. You can't possibly stop them all."

Billy Dee rubbed his hands together briskly. "Ma'am, we don't intend to stop them all. Just the Congressman and his party."

I started to feel light-headed. What with Susannah and Freni to deal with on a daily basis, I had all the conflict I cared to handle. I was also feeling duped, an emotion which in me inevitably leads to anger. I clutched the edge of the counter with both hands, closed my eyes, and slowly counted to ten. First in English, then in German. Then I took a deep breath and opened my eyes.

Billy Dee Grizzle was still there. To his credit, he looked concerned. "You all right, ma'am?"

"I'm as fine as frog hair," I snapped. "You, Mr. Grizzle, seem like a fair-enough guy. Why couldn't you have been up-front?" Of course I knew the answer, but what difference does that make?

Billy Dee might have been just a little embarrassed to defend his reprehensible actions, because he looked away when he answered. "Ma'am, sometimes the end does justify the means."

I took a deep breath and exhaled slowly through my nose. Living with Susannah had taught me how to control hyperventilation. To a point. "Not if the end involves my ruination, it doesn't."

He looked back at me. If Billy Dee's green eyes were the window to his soul, he had a far kinder soul than he let on. "Ma'am, we won't be doing any of our protesting at your place. I can promise you that. It's gotta be done out where the action is. We can't protest what they're about to do, or have already done. We gotta protest them actually doing it. Otherwise it don't count."

"That's a relief," I said with perhaps a trace of sarcasm. "I suppose that after you protest you'll all gather back here for an evening of parlor games?"

Billy Dee flashed another one of his big, white-toothed

smiles. "Sounds like fun, ma'am. Especially if you'd care to join us. Seriously, ma'am, we won't be causing you no trouble. I'll keep an eye on things myself."

"The only trouble, Mr. Grizzle, is that there is someone else trying to keep an eye on things around here. An interested third party, you might say. A reporter."

Billy Dee's smile seemed to shrink just a little. "A reporter? Are you sure? For which paper?"

"Does it really matter?" I asked, suddenly feeling very weary. When even one reporter latches on to something, it's like inviting the whole world in for tea. Of course, this had been beneficial to me when that one reporter wrote that rave review of the Inn. But I could well imagine what could happen if Miss Brown got caught up in the middle of the fracas that seemed inevitable between these two factions.

"Of course it matters, ma'am," said Billy Dee emphatically. "I know a lot of reporters, and maybe I'll be able to talk some sense into this one. You know, a little man-to-man talk." He either winked or had an erratic tic.

"I doubt whether Miss Brown is a candidate for a man-to-man talk."

"Miss Brown? Which paper did you say she was with?"

"I didn't. I mean, I'm not exactly sure." Already I'd done too much blabbing about one of the guests. If Susannah had done that, I'd be furious.

"Well, don't you worry none anyhow, ma'am," said Billy Dee kindly. "Like I said, I'll keep an eye on things and see that they don't get outta hand."

I put Miss Brown out of my mind and took Billy Dee's word, and his credit card, and then showed him to his room. Despite the fact that he was a little rough around the edges, he was really a very pleasant man. Although he laughed a lot, he was always polite, which of course goes a long way to making up for such frivolous behavior. But don't get me wrong. I was not interested in Billy Dee as a man. I'm sure he wasn't even a Mennonite. Besides which, I really don't have time for such considerations, not with the Inn to run, and Susannah to look out for. Those days are comfortably behind me.

After I dropped Billy Dee off at his room, I stopped by the kitchen to see how Freni was doing. "How's dinner coming along?" I asked cheerfully.

Freni was busy greasing loaf pans for the bread she was making, but she took time out of her busy schedule to glare at me. "I put dill seed in the bread dough. Does that make it whole grain or vegetable?"

I ignored her logic. "Another meat-eater just checked in," I said encouragingly.

"So, what's the score now?"

"Meat-eaters four, veggies three."

"And I grated some cheese into the dumpling batter, so you've got another fruit now," she said matter-of-factly. Clearly the woman was trying to be helpful.

"Where's Mose?" I asked. Usually at this time of day he could be found in the kitchen giving his wife a hand.

"Milking."

"Still?" With just two cows now, the afternoon milking should have been done over an hour ago.

Freni slathered grease into another loaf pan. "He's not doing the milking. One of the guests is."

"Which one?"

Freni shrugged. "All the English look alike to me." To Freni and Mose, anyone not Amish, or distinctly Mennonite, was an outsider, an "English" person. Even Susannah was English, now that she wore makeup and sleeveless dresses.

"Is the guest male or female?"

Freni gave me a look that, if harnessed, could have shriveled a bushel of apricots on a rainy day. "This is my Mose we are talking about, Magdalena. You watch your tongue. The guest was a very tall man. Skinny, like a clothesline pole."

"Ah, Joel Teitlebaum."

"A nice man," she added with surprising generosity.

Just then I noticed that the shortening Freni was using to grease the loaf pans was not vegetable shortening but lard she had rendered herself. "That's not vegetable!" I cried.

"It isn't meat," she retorted.

"But it comes from a pig!" Vegetarianism and cholesterol issues aside, I doubted Mr. Teitlebaum would have been thrilled if he knew its source.

"Grease is grease," said Freni stubbornly. "What matters is that the bread doesn't stick."

"What matters," I said tersely, "is that we are honest with our guests. Not to mention with ourselves."

"What was that?"

"Nothing."

"Would you like to do the cooking yourself?" Freni always asked me that question three seconds before she threatened to quit.

"You're a superb cook!" I said and fled from the room with one second to go.

If I had been thinking clearly, not rattled by the conflux of hunters and A.P.E.S., I would have dashed into Hernia and picked up some fresh vegetables at the supermarket. Then I would have made a huge salad and everyone would have been satisfied. The English love their iceberg lettuce. It seems almost to have a pacifying effect on them.

Personally, I'm not much on eating raw green leaves. The fact that you have to put stuff on it in order to make it palatable, seems absurd to me. Why not just down the stuff straight from the bottle and leave the leaves to the rabbits? But this is only my opinion. And if I had been less opinionated, and more accommodating, there might not have been a corpse clutching Mama's Dresden Plate quilt.

# Chapter Four

The new dining room occupies the entire bottom portion of the new wing. It is actually much more than a dining room. In one corner there is a half-finished quilt stretched across a sturdy oak frame. Guests are invited to try their hand applying a few neat stitches. Of course, if their needlework is lousy, Freni or I will rip out the stitches within moments of their checking out. I do, after all, sell the quilts in some of the trendiest gift shops along the East Coast.

If quilting's not their thing, guests can always try spinning or weaving in the other back corner of the vast room. Neither Freni nor I knows anything about either of these two pursuits, although some of the guests appear to be rather proficient at it. One two-week guest spun and wove a very attractive scarf, which I in turn sold for fifty dollars at our own little gift shop by the front desk.

I must admit there isn't much for men to do in the way of indoor activities, so I always suggest they shuck corn. For that purpose I keep a bushel basket of tasseled corn beside each of the armchairs that ring the back fireplace. Except for the odd ear, the men never shuck any. It seems that they much prefer to nap after Freni's meals, than engage in any kind of activity. Any kind. Or so their wives sometimes confide to me.

We do, of course, actually eat in the dining room. The single, solid oak table that stretches almost two thirds of the length of the room is the same table we used when Susannah and I were growing up. It was built by my great-grandfather Jacob "The Strong" Yoder from a tree that occupied the site of the original farmhouse. This table can seat twenty people comfortably, twenty-six in a pinch. Incidentally, Jacob "The Strong" and his wife, Magdalena, had sixteen children and forty-seven grandchildren.

But enough of my family history. My point is that all the guests eat at the same table. I sit at my rightful place at the head of the table, which just happens to be the end nearest the kitchen door, and Susannah takes her rightful place at the foot. If she happens to be home.

Freni and Mose do not eat with us. Even if Freni could countenance supping with the English, her sensitivities would never allow her to watch them eat her food. Or not eat it, as the case may be. Freni and Mose live in what is called a "grandparents house" on their youngest son's farm, which is really only a stone's throw from here if you take the shortcut. They eat a late supper there. Although I am tempted to digress further and tell you a little about their rather strange relationship with this son, it really isn't your business, is it? Or mine, for that matter.

At any rate, it seems to work out fairly well, having the guests eating together at the same table at the same time.

Nobody ever feels lonely, although a few people have complained about feeling snubbed. But then, you can't have everything, can you? Of course, I'm the one who determines the seating arrangement. It wouldn't do for perfect strangers to plop themselves down just anywhere. I at least know a little bit about each one, and I try to maximize compatibility. So just ignore Susannah's complaints.

Speaking of which, Susannah is supposed to help me set the table, but I usually end up doing it all myself. I keep it simple. I don't use tablecloths. It's not that I'm theologically opposed to tablecloths, but you wouldn't believe the way some of our guests eat! Money does not equate with manners. If I used tablecloths I'd have to spend most of my time doing laundry, which is no way to run a business. Besides, not only does the bare, plank table seem authentically Amish, but the splinters it imparts go a long way to keeping elbows off the table.

Of course we use dishes. I will admit, however, that I am a little tight-fisted when it comes to shelling out for crockery. What is the point of using bone china when the guests are expecting to eat off hand-thrown clay pottery? Believe me, the ironstone I originally picked up at the Woolworth's in Somerset, and have been supplementing from garage sales ever since, works just fine.

And is it my fault if people assume that I, or one of many relations, made the stuff? I was not trying to be devious when I put tape over the manufacturer's name on the back. I merely needed someplace to write "Property of the PennDutch Inn."

Guests never quite know what to expect when it comes to their first meal at the Inn; still, I do my best not to disappoint them. Atmosphere is what they're paying for, and atmosphere is what I give them. If I had my way, I'd begin each meal with everyone holding hands and bowing their heads for a prayer. After meals I would read the Bible to them, in German of course, and we'd sing a few ancient Swiss hymns. But not even Susannah would sit still for that.

Instead, I have to content myself with hostessing stuff. I greet each of the guests as they officially enter the dining room for the first time and take them to their seat. Normally I would speak to them in my fake German accent, which is frankly quite charming.

But on this particular day, the one just prior to deer-hunting season, I was in a quandary. Thanks to the rude Congressman, Garrett Ream, and the huffy Ms. Parker, my guests all knew my accent was a fake. The question now was whether or not I should resume this quaint affectation, or talk like the English. Reluctantly I decided to abandon my cultural heritage. Susannah, I knew, would be relieved.

"Good evening," I said pleasantly to Mrs. Ream, who was the first person to enter the dining room. People of her breeding are precise about time. "Allow me to show you to your seat."

Lydia Ream smiled her appreciation and followed obediently. "The Congressman and Mr. James will be down shortly. They're taking a call."

I seated Lydia to my immediate left. I had every reason to trust her table manners and I wanted to get a better look at her dress. I have never had to institute a dress code at the Inn, because people of this ilk generally conform to acceptable standards. However, seldom do they dress as swank and spiffy as Lydia Johns Ream.

I guess you would call it a ball gown. It was floor-length,

made of some kind of taffeta, and in front it was cut low enough to cause a chest cold. It was also bright red, a color our mother had always forbidden Susannah and me to wear for modesty's sake. Mrs. Ream was also wearing jewelry. Real jewelry. Diamonds and rubies and things.

"You look very nice," I said. I meant it.

"Thank you. I hope I haven't overdressed."

Thankfully, just then Ms. Parker strode into the room followed by her young protégée, Linda McMahon. I scurried to meet them, but before I could intercept them they had settled themselves at the far end of the table. Linda had seated herself on the far end, opposite Lydia's side, and Jeanette was seated at the very end, right in Susannah's chair.

"Good evening," I said perfunctorily, and then cut right to the chase. "This end seat is reserved."

"There is no card or sign to indicate that." Jeanette Parker did not display the slightest intention of moving.

"Actually, we have no need for cards, because all the seating is done by me, your hostess."

Linda stood up, but Jeanette remained rooted to Susannah's chair. Perhaps literally so. She was, after all, wearing a homespun cotton pajama outfit that was dyed a very pale shade of green. Had it not been for her flaming orange hair, she would have looked for all the world like a giant rutabaga. Of course most rutabagas don't talk.

"Ms. Yoder," said this rutabaga, "I just about broke my neck coming down those impossibly steep stairs of yours, not to mention that I pinched a nerve in my lower vertebrae trying to nap on that hideous thing you call a mattress. The fact that I can sit at all is something of a miracle. Is it really so necessary that I move, now that I've finally gotten comfortable?"

"Yes," I said and turned to greet Joel Teitlebaum and Billy Dee Grizzle, who had appeared at the door. I may never be a mother, but twenty-two years of teaching Sunday School at Beech Grove Mennonite Church have taught me how to deal with children.

"Evening, ma'am," said Billy Dee cordially. He had changed from a plaid to a plain denim shirt, which was the perfect foil for the rather attractive bola tie he was wearing.

"Good evening," I said just as pleasantly, and then for his ears only I whispered, "Don't worry. The reporter doesn't take meals with us."

Billy Dee nodded, and I turned my attention to Joel Teitlebaum.

If possible, Joel Teitlebaum was looking even taller and skinnier than he had before. He was wearing corduroy slacks, a striped shirt, and a narrow striped tie, which undoubtedly accounted for it. And although it might have been just my imagination, it seemed to me that his color had improved. Milking must have agreed with him.

"How did you like milking?" I asked. Frankly, I found it strange that someone who didn't drink milk on principle, would be interested in such an activity.

Joel's color improved even more when he blushed. "Actually, I didn't go milking after all. I decided to nap instead. But Mose, I mean Mr. Hostetler, said he'd let me help him tomorrow."

"I see," I said. Actually I didn't. Not only was there far too much napping going on, but an hour of Mose's time was now unaccounted for. Unless he'd been napping as well. Either way, it was best Freni not find out about it.

I seated Joel to the left of Linda, who had scooted up one chair to make room for Jeanette. They were, after all, roughly the same age, and undoubtedly knew each other, since they were both conspirators for A.P.E.S.

Billy Dee, however, posed a problem. If I put him down on the far end, on the other side of Susannah, my sister would just make a fool of herself. I couldn't very well move him next to Lydia and have him come between her and her husband, could I? So I took the only option I had left and put him on my immediate right, next to Joel. My intentions were entirely pure, I assure you.

Fortunately we didn't have to wait much longer for Congressman Ream and Delbert James. But no sooner did they step into the room than both men appeared to do a double take. It was as if they had accidentally entered the wrong room and were flustered at their mistake.

"This is the right place," I assured them with a laugh. Unfortunately my laughs can sound pretty phony when I'm irritated. Or so says Susannah.

Delbert at least displayed the good manners to apologize for his tardiness. I graciously accepted his apology and seated him down by Susannah, opposite Jeanette. It would be interesting to see if the two of them made a pitch for the man. Although his type didn't appeal to me personally, he was certainly a dapper man, pale pink dress shirt notwithstanding.

As for Congressman Ream, of course I seated him next to his wife, to the right of Delbert James. Like his wife, he had dressed formally for dinner. Although he did cut a handsome figure in his dinner jacket and bow tie, he was not nearly as impressive as his wife. Then again, one is never quite dressed without good manners, I always say.

Even I was about to give up on Susannah when she came swirling into the room. I might have known. My baby sister must have caught a glimpse of the elegant Mrs. Ream and decided to outdo her. Not that she could, of course. To my knowledge Susannah does not own any ball gowns, much less expensive jewelry. She does, however, possess a first-class imagination.

If Mama could have foreseen Susannah's outfit, she would have put off dying for another twenty years. "Outfit" is the only word I can use to describe what my sister was wearing. It was definitely neither a dress nor a pants suit. It was definitely hot pink, and sheer enough to strain soup through. It was both billowing and confining. Parts of it trailed behind her like streamers in the wind, yet in a few critical areas there didn't seem to be enough of it at all. And as if that weren't enough, Susannah had accessorized her creation with five pounds of cheap glass jewelry and a pound or two of makeup. Had I not smelled the cheap scent of her perfume, I would not have known at first who it was.

"You're late," I whispered as she flowed by.

Susannah didn't even glance my way. She was far too busy noticing that Billy Dee was not seated down at her end of the table. This made her scowl, until she noticed Delbert James. With a great flutter of fabric, Susannah settled herself in the chair vacated by Jeanette.

I rang the little brass bell in front of my place. Up until then there was no food on the table except pickled eggs and beets, and the dill seed bread. Of course I am not counting such items as butter and apple butter, which some of us consider a fruit. Or the four large pitchers of fresh-from-the-barn milk. At any rate, it didn't take long for Freni and Mose to appear, each bearing a steaming tureen. I directed Mose to put his down at Susannah's end of the table, and Freni at mine. Then they both stepped back a few paces, as if awaiting orders.

I peeked into the nearest tureen and smiled happily. At last Freni had listened to reason and followed my latest instructions. "The tureen in front of me contains traditional Amish chicken and dumplings," I announced proudly. "And of course some vegetables," I added pointedly. Everyone appeared to be listening intently. "For those of you with special dietary needs," I went on, "Mrs. Hostetler has prepared a meatless version, there in the other tureen."

A glance at Freni told me that she was pleased I had acknowledged her effort.

"Does the meatless version contain dairy products?" asked Jeanette, without even so much as lifting the lid and appreciating the wonderful aroma of Freni's cooking.

"Or eggs?" inquired the soft-voiced Linda.

From the corner of my eye I could see Freni frowning.

"Well, does it?" demanded Jeanette.

Congressman Ream didn't even seem to notice there was a conversation going on. "When do we get to see the wine list?" he asked.

Susannah giggled and I scowled. Both at her and the Congressman. "This establishment does not serve alcohol. That was made quite clear in the brochure," I reminded him.

Garrett Ream looked first at his aide, then his wife for confirmation. Both of them were nodding. "Helluva way to start off the hunting season," he muttered.

I did my best to transform my scowl into a glare. "Neither does this establishment tolerate bad language."

Susannah giggled again, and whispered something to Delbert.

"Well, are there eggs and dairy products in that concoction, or not?" Jeanette was not nearly as distractable as I had hoped.

"Mrs. Hostetler uses only fresh, organic ingredients in all of her cooking," I stalled. It wasn't much of a stall.

"Yes or no?" demanded Jeanette. She was standing up now, the purple red of her face clashing with the orange of her hair.

"No," I said quickly. "Of course not." Undoubtedly my own face was as red as Jeanette's. I could just feel the shame. I am not used to lying, and it actually hurts each time I have to do it.

Jeanette opened the tureen then and studied its contents. "You know, Ms. Yoder, I am not trying to be purposefully difficult here. I only ask these questions because I have to. It's been twelve years since I've eaten any eggs or dairy products, and in that time I've developed an allergic reaction to them."

I swallowed hard and stole another glance at Freni. Freni wasn't flinching.

"If you haven't eaten eggs or dairy products in twelve years, then how the hell—sorry, Ms. Yoder—can you tell you've developed an allergic reaction to them?" growled the Congressman.

His wife, bless her soul, immediately opened the tureen in front of her and made a great show of smelling the steam that rose from the huge container. "It smells absolutely delish. I simply must get your recipe."

I smiled gratefully, and for the next few minutes busied myself serving out portions from the pot containing chicken to the carnivores gathered around the table. Susannah, a card-carrying carnivore herself, obediently did her part by serving the herbivores from the tureen in front of her. At last we all dug in.

"First-class cooking, ma'am," said Billy Dee, while his mouth was still full. There were murmurs of agreement from the carnivores, and none of the herbivores so much as gagged or spit their food out. Freni smiled broadly.

"I think my grandmother was Pennsylvania Dutch," volunteered Delbert James proudly.

Susannah recoiled in mock horror. "Your secret's safe with us." There were the usual obliging laughs.

"Did I hear you say you were a hunter, sir?" Joel Teitlebaum politely asked the Congressman.

Garrett Ream put down his fork and studied the young man across from him. "Yes, I am. Congressman Garrett Ream."

"Joel Teitlebaum, sir. From Philly. Not exactly in your district."

"Are you a hunter, Mr. Teitlebaum?"

"I'm a sculptor, sir. I—"

"And you?" asked Garrett Ream, turning to Billy Dee.

"Billy Dee Grizzle. I'm a contractor."

Garrett Ream nodded impatiently "Do you hunt?"

"Used to," said Billy Dee. "Squirrel, pheasant, deer, you name it."

"I see," said the Congressman sarcastically. "What we have here is a reformed hunter then?"

Billy had just taken a big bite, so he merely nodded.

"Ever shoot boar?"

Billy answered with his mouth full. "Yep. Lots of boar hunting in Texas."

"What part of Texas?" I asked. Cousin Anna Kauffman married a Methodist and moved to Houston in 1974. I hadn't heard from her since.

"San Antone," said Billy Dee proudly. He turned back to the Congressman. "I've given up hunting now. But boar hunting was my favorite. More exciting than hunting deer."

"At least the boar stand a small chance," said Jeanette. "Deer are just sitting ducks." A couple of people laughed at her inadvertent joke, and I am ashamed to say I was among them.

"They don't stand much of a chance in Morocco," said the Congressman. "There they have beaters that drive them down out of the mountains, while the hunters wait in blinds to pick them off."

"We were lucky enough to be included in a royal hunting party once," explained Lydia, "by King Hassan of Morocco. The Atlas Mountains are exquisite in April."

"We killed over four hundred that day," said the Congressman proudly. "Stacked them up like a cord of firewood. Of course there were about fifty of us, including His Majesty. Best experience of my life."

"It sounds utterly disgusting," said Jeanette. "I can't believe you're actually proud of such a barbaric act."

"What is a boar, anyway?" asked Linda.

"A sort of wild pig," answered Delbert James. "With tusks."

"Were you in the hunt too?" asked Susannah.

"Not exactly. The hunt was just for Congressmen and

their wives. But I got to do some pretty special skiing that morning up on the higher slopes. Morocco has some first-rate runs."

"I ski," said Susannah. "Up at Seven Springs." That was news to me.

"I'd love to travel," I couldn't help saying. Not that anybody heard me. As soon as I opened my mouth, Jeanette opened hers and began to sputter. "There is chicken fat in this broth!"

I turned around to look at Freni, but both she and Mose had disappeared. "There couldn't be," I said, then, "Are you sure?"

"There are goblets of fat glistening on my plate. What would you call that?" demanded Jeanette.

"Gross," shuddered Linda.

Just then Shnookums, who had been hidden somewhere within Susannah's billowing costume, began to yip pitifully. Of course nobody else there, with the exception of Billy Dee, had the slightest clue what was going on.

"You may be excused," I said sharply to Susannah. "A little bicarbonate, and you should be as good as new by tomorrow."

My glare must have been as withering as I had intended it to be, because Susannah got up and left without another word.

"Well?" Jeanette persisted.

"Pass me the tureen," I said as calmly as I could. When it arrived, I examined and sampled its contents as objectively as I could. Frankly, the supposedly meatless dish was less tasty than the one that I knew contained chicken. This confirmed my belief that there was indeed a difference between the two dishes. On the other hand, there definitely were little golden bubbles of something floating in the broth and clinging to the dumplings and stewed vegetables.

"Well?" demanded Jeanette.

"I think I'm going to be sick," said Joel. His face had taken on the same rutabaga green as Jeanette's clothes.

"It's probably just corn oil," said Lydia soothingly. "Even Julia cooks with corn oil."

I beamed at her. I didn't know who Julia was, and I was sure Lydia had never seen the inside of a kitchen herself, but I was grateful for her help. Encouraged, I rang the little brass bell again.

Freni misunderstood and when she reappeared she was carrying an apple pie in each hand. I quickly took the pies from her. "Freni," I kept my voice low, "didn't you follow my instructions?"

Freni looked as if I had slapped her. "You told me to serve one with meat, and one without meat in it, Magdalena, and that's exactly what you got."

"There, you see!" I said triumphantly, turning to the others, who had undoubtedly heard our conversation anyway. "That tureen is entirely vegetarian."

"Tastes good, too," said Billy Dee, who had helped himself to a sample dumpling. "Mighty fine cooking."

Freni beamed. "This vegetarian cooking isn't so hard after all," she confessed. "Just cook like regular, and then rinse off the stuff that you want to be vegetarian."

Joel immediately covered his mouth with his napkin and fled from the room.

Jeanette Parker uprooted herself from her chair and stood. I hadn't realized how tall she was. From where I sat she seemed to tower over the table like a pale green monolith. "This is a breach of contract, Ms. Yoder," she shouted. "When word gets out—and it will—of your duplicity in this matter, you can kiss your cozy little inn good-bye. And you," she said, pointing a long and heavily ringed finger at Freni, "are a menace and disgrace to your profession. What were you trying to do, kill me with animal toxins?" She pushed her chair roughly aside and strode from the room.

"She didn't really mean that," said Linda softly, and scurried after her mentor.

"Don't worry, Miss Yoder," said Lydia Ream kindly. "You are under no obligation to meet the dietary needs of your guests. Just to supply them with ample food. Isn't that right?" She turned to the two men on her side of the table for confirmation.

"Yes, dear," said the Congressman, but it was obvious he didn't want to get involved.

"Mrs. Ream is absolutely right," said Delbert James a little more kindly.

That made me feel a bit better, but still I was fit to be tied. I had to take out my frustration on someone. "Freni," I said through clenched teeth, "you're fired." Then quickly I recanted, lest Freni take me seriously. There were just too many guests to go it on my own.

But it was too late. "I quit anyway," she snapped, before stomping from the room.

Now before you get too upset, I have to mention that Freni had already been fired more than once, and in fact she quits on the average of once every other week. Still, if I had been slower to anger that last day before deer-hunting season, there might not have been a corpse clutching Mama's Dresden Plate quilt. Then again, there might well have been anyway.

# Chapter Five

## FRENI HOSTETLER'S
## CHICKEN AND DUMPLING RECIPE
*Serves 8*

2 chickens (year-old hens preferred)
1 ½ teaspoons salt
Dash black pepper
6 medium-size potatoes (quartered)
3 large carrots (sliced)
1 large onion (chopped)
4 tablespoons chopped parsley

3 cups flour
1 teaspoon salt
3 teaspoons baking powder
Dash ground nutmeg
3 eggs, beaten
½ cup cream

Clean and pluck the hens. Give head, entrails, and feet to barn cats. Do what you want with the liver, stomach, and gizzard. Cut the hens into serving pieces and put them into a large, cast-iron pot. Sprinkle with salt and pepper and cover with water. Cook slowly until almost tender. Then skim off excess fat and foam that has formed on top. Add vegetables and cook 20 minutes more. Then spoon dumpling batter on top of boiling broth and meat. Cover kettle tightly and cook 10 more minutes. Do not open the kettle until ready to serve.

To make dumplings, sift the dry ingredients together. Then add the beaten eggs and enough cream to make a batter stiff enough to drop from a spoon.

# Chapter Six

With Freni gone, it meant that I had to wash the supper dishes by myself—since I had banished Susannah to her room. Not that I minded. I find that immersing my hands in hot water is soothing whenever I, myself, am metaphorically in hot water. If my hands can stand it, so can I.

I surely did not expect company at the kitchen sink, and would almost have preferred not to have it. But it never pays to be rude to paying guests. Especially when they are trying to be kind.

"Where do you keep the dish towels?" asked Lydia merrily. She had changed out of her ball gown and into a casual, pink cashmere sweater and natural linen slacks.

I opened a drawer and took out a stack of neatly folded towels. "I may have to charge you extra for the privilege," I said, only half-seriously.

"Slumming it, are we?" asked Delbert James, appearing in

the doorway. He too had changed, or at least shed the tie and coat.

Lydia seemed to light up like a well-trimmed wick touched to flame. "I was hoping it was going to be just us girls," she practically cooed. It was embarrassingly obvious she was hoping anything but that.

I swallowed my surprise for the third time and handed them each a towel. "Stack the dried dishes on that counter. I'll put them away myself. But you can hang the pots on those pegs over there."

"Aye, aye, Captain," said Delbert. Without the tie, or maybe it was without the Congressman, he was a different person altogether.

"I suppose this is a first for both of you," I teased. Well, maybe probed.

Delbert chuckled. "Not for me. Not by a long shot. I put myself through Northwestern washing dishes. Four years of journalism paid for with dishpan hands."

"You're a journalist by training?"

"Speech writer, actually."

"That's very interesting. My sister, Susannah, has always wanted to be a writer. But fiction, not speeches."

"Is there a difference?" asked Lydia.

We all laughed. "What exactly does a Congressman's aide do?" I asked.

"Besides speech writing," said Delbert, "just about everything. On this trip, I even act as gun-bearer."

"So only the Congressman hunts?"

"I hunt," said Lydia. There seemed to be pride in her voice. "Daddy took me with him on safari in Africa when I was just a little girl. Of course, that was back in the old days, before we gave much thought to conservation." She paused and gave me a slightly challenging look. "Deer hunting in Pennsylvania is a different story altogether."

"Of course," I agreed. I did understand. There are many more deer in the state now than there were when the first white settlers showed up. Every year over a thousand deer are killed by cars on our county's highways alone. Not that I could ever kill one intentionally myself, although I have had the urge from time to time when I find them in my garden.

"Lydia, I mean, Mrs. Ream, is a first-class shot," said Delbert. He lowered his voice. "She can outshoot the Congressman any day."

Lydia laughed and flicked Delbert playfully with her towel. I looked discreetly away. I generally try to ignore my guests' shenanigans, which doesn't mean, of course, that I approve of them. It's just that I have all I can handle in Susannah. "I aim to bag the biggest buck around," she said, imitating Billy Dee's accent.

"Does it bother you that we have A.P.E.S. staying at the Inn?" I asked. It was more of a warning than a question. I genuinely liked Lydia and didn't want to see her tackled by the likes of Jeanette Parker.

"What?"

"She means," said Delbert, solemnly folding his dish towel, "that Billy Dee and the rest all belong to an organization called the Animal Parity Endowment Society. They're philosophically and morally opposed to the taking of any animal's life. They are especially against hunting for sport."

Lydia's face suddenly lost its animation. Where just a moment before, she had appeared relaxed and surprisingly youthful, now it was as if she had just donned a mask of well-bred inscrutability. It did not suit her nearly as well. "I see," she said. Even her diction had changed. "And how long have you known this, Delbert?"

Delbert cleared his throat before answering. "The Congressman and I both recognized Ms. Parker and Ms. McMahon when we entered the dining room tonight. Both of them have been up on the Hill a number of times lobbying for their cause."

"And the other two? Mr. Grizzle and the sculptor from Philadelphia?"

"Garrett," he looked at me, "I mean, the Congressman, suspected they might be part of the organization as well. That's why he asked those questions about hunting at supper. A quick call afterward confirmed it. Mr. Grizzle has been a member for three years. Mr. Teitlebaum, the sculptor, for almost seven. They're all here together, and as far as we know they intend to disrupt our plans for tomorrow."

"You knew about this?" asked Lydia. The question was directed to me, and sounded stingingly like an accusation.

The most valuable lesson I ever learned from Papa was to stick up for myself with confidence. Especially if I had done nothing wrong. We Mennonites may be pacifists, but we're not pushovers. "Everyone has to use the six-seater," Papa used to say, "and it all ends up in the same big hole." The six-seater was our outhouse, and most of our family's quality-time was spent around that one big hole. Of course, we now have indoor plumbing, along with telephones in every room. Incidentally, our six-seater is still the biggest outhouse in the county.

"I most certainly did not know about this. Not when I booked this week's reservations. It wasn't until Billy Dee arrived, and he was the last one, I might add, that I found out. He told me himself."

Lydia's mask was still tightly in place. "And how long were you going to keep this information to yourself? Until after the reporters got involved and you got yourself some more coverage for the Inn?"

That raised even my pacifist hackles. The PennDutch does not need any additional coverage. Certainly not coverage of confrontation over controversial causes. "And just how long were your husband and his aide going to keep their discovery from you? I am, after all, the one who clued you in, not them."

The mask slipped a trifle. "I'm sorry, Miss Yoder. I apologize. You do have a point."

Never miss out on an opportunity to kick a dead horse; it is, after all, a form of exercise. I was tempted to tell Lydia there already was a reporter on the premises, and I had yet to spill one solitary bean of information to her. Wisely, though, I concluded that rubbing Lydia's nose in my discretion would be more trouble than it was worth. Instead, I decided to accept her apology. People hate it when you forgive them.

"I forgive you," I said.

Lydia's face assumed the color of one of Freni's pickled beets. "Now, if you'll excuse me, I have some matters to take care of." She carefully put down her dish towel, and then, with the regal bearing of a queen, departed my humble kitchen. Delbert immediately chased after her, like a faithful dog. Of course he was of a breed much larger and quieter than Shnookums's.

I finished up the dishes by myself. The hot water was as therapeutic as ever. When I pulled the plug and watched the last of the water swirling down the drain, I imagined my troubles were the food particles caught up in the vortex. Starting with Jeanette Parker, and ending up with Lydia Johns Ream, the whole shebang of them, Susannah and her mutt included, swirled out of sight, and temporarily out of mind. Very temporarily. I was still wiping out the sink when the Congressman himself paid me a visit.

"Miss Yoder!"

I whirled, clutching my wet towel defensively to my bosom. Not since Crazy Maynard Miller exposed himself at my window one night have I felt so frightened. Or so guilty.

"Yes!"

The Congressman had been standing right behind me, and when I turned, he nearly poked me in the eye with his righteously extended forefinger. Seeing him so close, I yelped involuntarily. Unfortunately there was no room for me to back up. I flattened my buttocks against the still-warm sink.

"Miss Yoder," he said through clenched teeth, "I am a patient man. A tolerant man. But I will not have people meddling in my business. Is that clear?"

I felt like I had when Mr. Lichty, my sixth-grade teacher, caught me doodling during long division. Although Garrett Ream and I were approximately the same age, the fact that he was a United States Congressman, an Episcopalian at that, and I a mere Mennonite innkeeper, made me feel about as equal to him as Shnookums must have felt to me. "Yes, sir. I understand," I said. But of course I didn't. What I said to his wife was my business, not his.

"It's bad enough that you booked those people during my hunting trip. But you had no right to scare Mrs. Ream with unnecessary information."

"I didn't mean to scare her. Just inform her."

"To what purpose?"

"To keep her from having to tangle with Jeanette Parker. It hasn't happened here yet, but I've read accounts of animal rights activists hassling hunters in other counties."

"I can take care of my own wife, thank you. And Ms. Parker."

"Well, excuuuuse me for caring," I said. It was the exact tone Susannah uses when she means anything but. I guess I'd had enough. Garrett Ream might have been a Congressman, but he had to use the six-seater just as often as the rest of us.

He backed away slightly, but I kept my fanny pressed up against the sink.

"Well, this wasn't the only thing I came down here to talk about," he said. He was decidedly less belligerent, so, in addition to onion on his breath, I could smell a favor coming on.

I said nothing. It was the first sense of power I'd felt all evening.

"You see," he hastened to explain, "in order for us to avoid any kind of confrontation with this group, we need to leave the hotel very early."

"That makes sense. Provided they don't follow you." I was sorely tempted to tell him that there was a reporter sacked out upstairs.

"You won't tell, will you?" It was more of an order than a question.

"I'm not the fool you take me for."

He smiled in an apparent attempt to smooth things over. "You are far from anybody's fool, Miss Yoder. If I had you on my staff, I'm sure the team would get a lot more done."

I didn't smile back. "I'm not looking for a job, Congressman. What is it exactly that you want?"

He sighed, a fake-sounding sigh of defeat, and ran his fingers through his thick, dark hair. "Just breakfast. An early breakfast—say fiveish, and box lunches for the three of us. And feel free to use meat." Then he laughed at his own little joke.

"Bacon and eggs for five at three—I mean, three at five. And ham and lettuce sandwiches to go. Anything else?"

"That you not tell my wife we had this little conversation."

"As you wish."

He left abruptly, without even as much as a thank you. As I watched him go, I realized that Congressman Garrett Ream no longer seemed so handsome as when he had checked in. His features may have been regular, maybe even classical in shape, but he was ugly just the same.

"Please close the door!" I called after him.

Of course he didn't. Wearily I started to make and pack the lunches he'd requested. As tired as I was, I'd be even more tired at five in the morning. That I knew.

# Chapter Seven

I stuck my head in the dining room before going off to bed. Guests are forever leaving lights on. A recent survey, conducted by yours truly, revealed that people use eight and a half times more electricity and water when staying at places other than their own homes. It is no coincidence, for example, that most of New York City's blackouts occur in the summertime, when the city is full of tourists.

Anyway, I stuck more than just my head into the dining room. At first I couldn't believe what I saw. There, sewing contentedly away on the stretched quilt, were Linda McMahon and Billy Dee Grizzle. It was like finding a cat and a mouse gnawing away at the same piece of cheese.

I approached them quietly, not stealthily. At five feet ten, and one hundred and fifty pounds, I am too big-boned to do anything stealthily. Still, I got close enough to discern Linda's soft, almost girlish voice.

"Of course I love her, Billy Dee. But that doesn't mean I

approve. Blackmail is blackmail. And besides, you can only push someone so far."

"She's pushed a lot of people too far, Linda. Someday someone's going to put a stop to it."

Linda looked up from her sewing with what appeared to be concern. "She apologized to you, Billy Dee. Publicly, even. Remember?"

Billy Dee chuckled, but it wasn't a happy sound. "Yes, she did apologize. After I 'found the light.' "

"But you did find the light. I mean, you did change. So now you can understand why she took the position she did, can't you?"

"Yeah, I guess, Linda. But it ain't her blackmailing that's bothering me now. We've got our own little problem to take care of."

Linda beat the stretched fabric of the quilt with both fists. "But it isn't a problem, Billy Dee. We've been over this a million times. I want to keep it!"

At that point I stubbed my right big toe on a chair, and since both the chair and I made a lot of noise, my presence was immediately evident. I covered the best I could.

"Sorry, I didn't mean to startle you two. I just popped in to see if you needed some help."

Much to my disappointment, they appeared neither to be startled, nor to need my help. "We're just fine, ma'am," said Billy Dee politely. "But you can check our stitches if you want."

I peered over his shoulder like a school marm and scrutinized his handiwork. Billy Dee, I concluded, was either a tailor or an ex-marine. His stitches were exemplary. As were Linda's.

If the two of them finished up the quilt, I stood a good chance of winning first prize at the county fair in August.

"I've seen worse," I said. It doesn't pay, you know, to praise people too highly. Not when you want more work out of them. Big egos lead to lazy fingers—that's what Mama always said.

"Thank you, Ms. Yoder," said Linda nonetheless. "This is actually a lot of fun."

"That's 'Miss,' " I reminded her, "not 'Mizz.' "

She giggled, brushed a strand of long, mouse-brown hair out of her eyes, and went back to work. When not in the presence of Jeanette Parker, she seemed pleasant enough. Perhaps she could be reasoned with as well.

"Ms. McMahon," I began hesitantly, "I am aware that you are a member of the Animal Parity Endowment Society, and I know why you're here."

Linda looked up at me with almost mocking sweetness. "And why is that?"

"To harass the Congressman and his wife, of course."

Linda flashed a not-so-sweet look at Billy Dee. "You told?"

He nodded. "It was just a matter of time, Linda. Subterfuge is not my strong point."

"Well, then, Miss Yoder, what is it you want?"

I swallowed hard before taking the big plunge. "I would like for you, I mean all of you, to keep your protest out of the Inn. I am a pacifist, you know."

Linda turned her gaze back to her work. "I can respect that, Miss Yoder. I really can. We are, after all, pacifists ourselves."

"Quakers?" I asked hopefully. Although I'm sure there must be some, I had never heard of a vegetarian Mennonite.

Linda giggled again. She was either a very good actress, or
as sweet as maple syrup. "I belong to the New Age Church of
Holistic Oneness, Miss Yoder. We don't believe in violence
either. Against humans—or animals. That's why we must protest the taking of innocent lives. In this case, deer lives. And
what better way to spread our gospel of inter-species coexis-
tence than to bring it to the attention of the media."

My throat felt dry. "Which media?" To my knowledge
Hernia only had a weekly paper.

Linda didn't miss a beat. I mean stitch. "The national
media, of course. ABC, CNN, you know the ones."

"I don't watch television," I said proudly. Actually, that
wasn't quite true. Occasionally when Susannah is out, I sneak
into her room and watch reruns of "Green Acres." "And besides which, why single out Congressman Ream? Tomorrow
there will be thousands of hunters out there."

"Sad, yet true. But how many of them are ambitious politi-
cians, who at the very least will attract media coverage and
who are in the position to introduce legislation outlawing this
barbaric pastime?"

"You have a point," I conceded, "but can you at least keep
the Inn out of it?"

Linda sighed the impatient sigh of the young. When Susannah, who is not so young anymore, does it, she rolls her
eyes as well. Linda, to her credit, kept her eyes on her work. "I
already told you, Miss Yoder, I respect your wishes. I do not
lie."

As long as she wasn't looking up, there was no harm in me
rolling my eyes, was there? "I believe you. But what about Miss
Parker? She's your leader, isn't she?"

Linda and Billy both laughed. "Ma'am," said Billy, who

did look up and almost caught me in mid-roll, "we A.P.E.S. don't have leaders. We do things by consensus. What Linda says goes for me as well. As I'm sure it will for Joel. So you don't have nothing to worry about, Miss Yoder. Except maybe getting a good night's sleep and finding yourself a new cook."

"Speaking of which," I said, "how does buckwheat pancakes with home-harvested honey sound for breakfast?" I was trying to be cooperative, I really was.

"Is the honey organic?" inquired Linda.

"The bees are especially bred to produce organic honey," I said, rolling my eyes again.

Billy Dee caught my look and winked. "Got any bacon to go with that?"

"Home-cured. Organic as well."

"Very funny," said Linda, still not looking up.

"Mr. Grizzle," I then said nervously, "may I please speak to you a moment out in the hall? It's about that problem with the toilet in your room."

Of course, there was nothing wrong with Billy Dee's toilet, and it was stupid of me to imply that there was. Susannah always says I add too many details to my lies. Sparse lies, she says, generally go across much better.

But Billy Dee was at least a cooperative conspirator. "Sure thing, Miss Yoder," he said hopping up. "I been meaning to talk to you about that myself."

"Did you get a chance to talk to Miss Brown?" I asked when we were alone.

"No, ma'am. I knocked on her door a couple of times, but either she ain't in, or she's out like a light. A lot of them reporters have drinking problems, you know."

I didn't know, but now I certainly hoped it was true. When

Susannah comes home in her cups, I can count on her sleeping for at least the next twelve hours. With any luck, and if what made Miss Brown's suitcase so heavy was booze, the retiring reporter might be out of commission for most of the week. Of course I am theologically, as well as personally, opposed to alcohol, but the good Lord is just as capable of using the devil's tools to his advantage as anything else.

"Say, Miss Yoder," added Billy Dee as an afterthought, "I'd like to do me a little pole fishing tomorrow evening when we get back. Any ponds around here?"

"Miller's pond is just up the road about a mile and a half. He doesn't mind if you fish it, as long as you close the cattle gate behind you."

"Sure thing, ma'am, thanks. But, say, you wouldn't happen to have an empty jar or something I could keep my bait in? You know, with a lid."

I refrained from laughing. "It's November, Mr. Grizzle. If you're looking for night crawlers, you may have to dig down to China."

"Name's Billy Dee, ma'am, remember? Anyhow, I bet that cow manure out there back of the barn keeps the ground as warm as toast. Might have to wrestle me those worms out of the ground, they'll be so big."

He was probably right. Papa used to fish in November, and with night crawlers too, I think. "I keep some empty jars in that old cabinet on the back porch. Help yourself. You need a flashlight?"

"Naw, but thank you, ma'am."

"Just turn out the lights when you leave."

At the rate they were working, the quilt might well be finished by the time they turned in.

. . .

By then I was pooped, so I headed circuitously for bed. We have no night clerk here at the PennDutch. There is no "vacancy" sign for me to turn on or off in the evenings. If all the guests have arrived, I am free to toddle off to bed whenever I feel like it. All the guests have their own keys to the front door and are free to come and go as they please. Once or twice I might get up in the middle of the night to see if the front door has been locked, but this is only a recent practice. I know every single solitary soul living in Hernia, even the three Baptists, and if it hadn't been for the rape and murder of Rachel Zook by an itinerate vagabond last year, I wouldn't bother to lock up at all.

After locking the front door, I turned off the lights in the main sitting room and then popped into the parlor. The parlor has always been the parlor. It too is located at the front of the house, just off the sitting room, and back when the sitting room used to be the dining room, the parlor was where we entertained the non-eating guests. Eating company, as Mama called the others, had no need to use the parlor. But for non-eating guests, the ones you only wanted to stay for an hour or less, the parlor was the perfect solution.

The parlor was smaller than the dining room but had a lot more personality. Although it had its own entrance off the front porch, we never used it but always entered through the old dining room. I think that in the very old days the parlor used to be the kitchen, because the wall opposite the dining room is dominated by an enormous hearth. The hearth is mostly filled in now with bookshelves, but the center portion has been kept open as a fireplace.

Back when Grandma ran the show, the parlor was furnished only with straight-back, uncomfortable chairs. Any visitor who managed to survive sitting in one for an hour without squirming was a candidate for elevation to an eating guest. But when Mama took over, she changed all the rules. Out went the straight-backs and in came the overstuffed. Comfy furniture was Mama's one concession to decadence.

I must confess that I have taken Mama's drastic changes a step further, by the addition of two Lazy Boy recliners. It was in one of these chairs that I found Joel Teitlebaum.

"Oh, good evening," I said. It had been an evening of surprises and I was a mite startled. I am, after all, easily lost in my thoughts.

"Good evening, Miss Yoder," Joel said cheerfully. He had apparently been reading one of the books from the hearth and munching on sunflower seeds. A little stack of empty shells lay on an end table next to him.

"Is it a good book?" I asked lamely. I am always at a loss when talking alone to a man, even one young enough to be my son.

"It's not bad. *Parallels and Discrepancies Between Amish and Orthodox Jewish Lifestyles* by Judith Hostetler Cohen. Is she related to your cook?"

"Somehow. And to me. Virtually all Hostetlers in the country are descendants of one man, Jacob Hochstetler, who immigrated to America from Switzerland in 1738. In fact, about eighty percent of all Amish are somehow related through this one man, as are heaps of Mennonites."

"Even Jeff Hostetler, the Giants' quarterback?"

"Yes." I knew nothing about football, but Susannah did, and Jeff Hostetler's kinship had already been established.

"Bad," said Joel.

"Pardon me?"

Joel smiled patiently. "Bad means good."

"So you didn't like the book then?"

Joel laughed. "No, the book was okay. 'Bad' and *'bad'* mean two different things."

"I see." Of course I didn't.

Joel held out a little brown sack of sunflower seeds and offered them to me. "Want some?"

"No, thanks. Are you still hungry?" There were plenty of raw carrots and apples in the kitchen I could offer him instead.

"Naw. I had some 'peach jerky' and kelp cookies up in my room. I hope you don't mind."

"Munch away," I said. "You are, after all, on the Amish Lifestyle Plan, so I trust you'll clean up all the crumbs." I wasn't worried anyway. Despite the fact that he was dressed in some homespun-looking fabric, and was wearing plastic sandals with navy blue socks, Joel Teitlebaum was impeccably neat.

"I hear that you've discovered our purpose for being here, Miss Yoder."

I sat down in the easy chair nearest him. "And how did you hear that?" I had left Billy and Linda safely in the dining room just minutes before.

He took some shells out of his mouth and started stacking up another neat pagoda. "I couldn't help hearing when I was in my room. The Congressman and his aide were in the hallway, and they didn't exactly keep their voices down. The Congressman, for one, seemed pretty ticked."

"What exactly did he say?"

"Enough to tell me that we're going to have to get up

pretty early in the morning to keep track of them." His tone was only slightly accusing.

"How early?"

"Just early. They didn't say when they planned to sneak out."

I breathed a sigh of relief. "I'll have a vegetarian breakfast all prepared for you by seven," I offered. I am a firm believer in at least postponing any confrontation that I can't stop.

"Can you make it six instead?"

"Six-thirty." I felt like I was bargaining away one of my quilts.

"Okay, I'll tell the others. Say, how much snow are we expecting by morning, anyway?"

"Not any that I know of. Why?" The last weather report I'd heard had called for fair skies with a low of thirty-eight and pockets of scattered frost in low-lying areas. Of course that forecast might have been from a week ago.

"I thought I heard the Congressman say something about snow." He glanced down at his plastic sandals. "I just didn't want to have to go tramping about in the snow in these things. They're the only shoes I brought with me. Got caught up in one of my sculptures and packed kind of quickly," he added sheepishly.

"If it does snow, I can lend you a pair of galoshes," I offered gallantly.

"But Miss Yoder," he said laughing, "I wear a size twelve. Men's twelve. I doubt if even your feet are that big."

"Thank you, sort of. But these aren't mine really—these were my father's."

"In that case, thank you. I'm sorry. I didn't mean to offend you."

"No offense taken. Well, speaking of feet, I'm dead on mine. If you want to tell the others about breakfast, young Linda and Mr. Grizzle are still in the dining room quilting away like they were at a bee."

"Linda and Billy?" He sounded genuinely surprised, but recovered quickly and said good night. I got the impression he would continue reading until milking time. Young people these days don't seem to need any sleep. It must be all that fluoride they've been getting in their water.

As I closed the door behind me, all I could think about was crawling into my warm, snuggly bed. Then I remembered that I was going to have to share my bed and choked back a yelp of dismay.

# Chapter Eight

If you've never had to share a bed with Susannah, count yourself lucky. I hate to say this about my own sister, but unfortunately each year fewer and fewer people can count themselves lucky. Of course I don't share Susannah's bed in the same way these people do, but, still, I feel a weird sort of bond with them.

If you survive the night with Susannah, chances are that you will emerge with enough bumps and bruises to draw looks of sympathy from total strangers, and undoubtedly will be a good deal deafer to boot. Susannah thrashes and snores like nobody's business. When Mama and Papa were alive, we had a sow named Susannah, and its name was no coincidence. It is a pure wonder that Susannah's precious little Shnookums sleeps with her every night and still survives. But perhaps this explains why the mutt is so high-strung he can catch kites on a windless day.

"Susannah," I warned her that night for the millionth time, "unless you want to sleep on the floor, stay on your side of the bed. And for pity's sake, sleep on your left side. Otherwise you sound like a pond full of bullfrogs."

Despite her claim to tiredness, Susannah had been awake and watching "Murder, She Wrote" on her portable TV. "Dishes done?" she'd asked callously when I entered the room. I said nothing and let her finish the program while I undressed. Just having the TV on, especially on a Sunday night, made me feel guilty.

"Well, if we're not going to be chatty, all right if I stay up and watch the movie? It's about this woman who finds out her husband's having an affair, and she decides to get even by having an affair of her own, except that the man she chooses is the husband of the woman her husband is having an affair with. So, at one point they figure it out and—"

That's when I made her turn off the TV and scoot over. "Susannah dear," I said, trying to imitate Mama's voice, "let's say our prayers now and get ready for the sandman."

"Is he cute?"

I simply refused to answer. Cute is not what Susannah is after. John Stutzman, who goes to our church, is cute, and he's all eyes for Susannah, but she pays him no mind. Not that Susannah goes to our church anymore anyway. My point is that Susannah is turning her back on our people and our traditions to such an extent that, as awful as it is to say so, I am glad Mama and Papa are not here to see it. That old adage about the apple not falling far from the tree is plain baloney. Susannah's apple rolled out of the orchard and into the world the year Mama and Papa died.

I eventually quit fuming about Susannah and fell asleep. Both she and Shnookums beat me to it, however, and when I did drift off, it was to the alternating rhythm of Susannah's deep throaty snores and Shnookums's pitiful pips. At some point I dreamed that I was stranded in a rowboat without oars in the world's largest frog pond. Maybe it was even an ocean, except that it was shallow enough for cattails and fresh enough for millions of croaking, squeaking, and bellowing frogs. Then, suddenly, all the frogs but one fell silent, and the one, in a startlingly human voice, began to scream for help.

I woke up and turned on the bedside lamp. Not surprisingly, Susannah and Shnookums were still sound asleep. Of course, it wasn't their dream, but not that it made any difference. It is those with the most on their consciences who sleep the soundest, or haven't you noticed? Anyway, I was just about to turn off the light and try to go back to sleep when I heard the scream again. This time I was definitely not dreaming.

I put on my slippers and threw on my heavy corduroy robe, which doesn't at all compromise my modesty, and set out to investigate. The scream seemed to have come from upstairs, possibly from the new wing, above the new dining room. As soon as I had negotiated the impossibly steep stairs, it was immediately clear that I was on the right track. Joel and all three members of the Ream party were standing in the hallway looking toward the new wing.

"What the—" began the Congressman, but I cut him off.

"It's okay, folks, I'll take care of this." I mean, what's the point of standing around and scratching your head when all you have to do is check something out?

The scream, a sort of garbled "help," was emitted one more time, and then I immediately knew where it came from. I headed straight for Susannah's old room, with Joel at my heels.

The door was open, and the reading lamps on either side of the bed were turned on. Centered in the bed, but with her back pressed up against the headboard, was Linda McMahon. She seemed to be staring fixedly at something on the quilt that covered her legs.

"Linda!" Joel pushed past me and raced to the bed.

"Help!" she screamed one more time. So intently was she staring at whatever it was, she didn't seem to be aware of our presence.

I went around to the other side of the bed and tried to follow the angle of her gaze. She was staring at something just below her knees, at some point in a strip of blue and red calico. Then I saw it too, but, I'm ashamed to say, I started to laugh.

"What's so funny?" demanded Joel.

"It's only this." I took off one of my slippers and laid it gently on the quilt, atop Linda's shins. When I removed it a minute later, there was a little brown, eight-legged creature clinging to it. "A little itsy-bitsy, teensie-weensie spider."

Joel recoiled as if I were waving a snake at him, and Linda somewhat ironically began to open and close her mouth like a baby bird begging to be fed.

"Come on, folks, get a grip on it," I said in my best Susannah imitation. "This is a harmless little house spider, just out to get himself a midnight snack. And I don't mean you," I hastened to assure Linda.

"Where did he come from?" Joel had backed far enough away from the bed so that I was having to lean way over it just to allow him to get a good look.

"Probably from up there," I said, pointing to the ceiling. "He really is harmless, I can assure you. He eats things too small to even see. In fact, some folks consider them to be lucky spiders." I wasn't really lying. Susannah did consider it lucky when I didn't make her sweep down all the cobwebs that eventually collected in her room.

"Well, I consider it a health hazard and a menace," said the Congressman, who had apparently been standing in the doorway for some time. "You will, of course, be calling an exterminator in the morning." It was a directive, not a question.

I simply stared at the Congressman in his peacock-blue silk robe, not quite sure what to say. At last the lovely Lydia intervened by slipping her arm through her husband's and pulling him gently away. "Come on, dear," I heard her say as she led him down the hall, "you've got to get some sleep if you're going to bag that eight-point buck in the morning." Wordlessly, their loyal aide trotted after them.

"What are you going to do about him?" asked Joel.

"Ignore him, I guess."

"No, I mean him." He pointed to the spider, which was still clinging to my slipper.

I glanced down at the little critter, which by then was crawling up the slipper toward my hand. "Open the window, please!"

"Oh, no," cried Joel. "You can't do that! It's November. Arachnids can't take freezing weather."

I headed resolutely for the bathroom.

"Not that, either, Miss Yoder." He took a couple of deep breaths and seemed to calm down a little. "I mean, please. Can't we release him someplace safe and warm?"

I practically thrust the slipper at him. "Here, you release him. Try the cellar—through the kitchen, but before the porch."

Joel took the slipper, handling it as gingerly as Susannah handles the poop-scoop on those rare occasions when she stoops to clean up after Shnookums. But once it was in his possession, he took off at a sprint.

I sat down on the edge of the bed to attend to young Linda. She had ceased gaping like a hungry fledgling and was by this time gasping like a dying fish. I patted her shoulder and tried to look sympathetic. Admittedly, nurturing is not my forte.

"There, there," I said somewhat lamely, "it'll be all right."

"But he might die down there," she finally managed to say.

"Don't worry," I hastened to assure her, "there are plenty more where that one came from."

Linda began gasping and gaping again, and it took me a couple of minutes to get her coherent. "Not the spider! Joel!"

I patted her a little harder. "Joel will be just fine. The cellar stairs aren't that much steeper than these, and Mose promised me he would fix both the loose steps."

"You idiot!" said Linda rudely. I must have looked shocked, because she almost immediately apologized. "But don't you see," she added, "poor Joel could get bitten by that horrible thing and die?"

I smiled kindly. "Absolutely not. That little spider couldn't even kill a fly. I've been bitten by them oodles of times. Of course it hurts, but all that happens is that you get a little lump that goes away in a couple of hours. Joel will be just fine."

As if on cue, Joel popped back into the room with my slipper in hand. "All's well that ends well," he said, perhaps a little out of breath.

"Thanks, Joel."

"No problem, Miss Yoder."

"Yeah, thanks, Joel." Linda seemed to be breathing normally again.

I figured it was a good time for me to leave. "Well, good night, then."

"Good night, Miss Yoder. I'll stay with her for a while."

Linda smiled appreciatively up at Joel. Perhaps I had been wrong about some of my early assumptions. "When you assume," Papa used to say, "you make an *ass* out of *u* and *me*."

I said my good nights and had just started down the hall when something occurred to me. I turned back. Both young people were just as I had left them. "Say," I said hesitantly, "isn't it a little odd that with all the commotion, Ms. Parker doesn't seem to have awakened?"

"Not at all," answered Linda. She sounded just a wee bit smug. "She usually takes a 'chill pill.'"

"A what?"

"A tranquilizer," translated Joel. He looked to Linda for confirmation.

She nodded. "Jeanette, I mean Ms. Parker, has a chronic back problem. It's exacerbated by stress. A Xanax now and then relaxes her and helps her get to sleep."

"I see," I said, but of course I didn't. I generally disapprove of any kind of medication. Oh, not on religious grounds, I assure you. It's just that Granny Yoder was a hypochondriac.

At one time I counted thirty-seven different bottles of pills and vitamins in her medicine chest. If the old lady had simply let nature take its course, she might have left the planet years earlier and spared us all a lot of grief.

I was coming out of Linda's room when I noticed that the fire escape door at the end of the new wing, right next to Miss Brown's room, was slightly ajar. My first thought was that the reclusive Miss Brown had slipped out for a breath of fresh night air. After all, moths are most active at night. But then I noticed a thin trail of sunflower seeds and concluded that young Joel was the insomniac I'd suspected him to be. I made a mental note to talk to him in the morning. If Crazy Maynard got in and showed young Linda what he showed me, she might scream for days.

On the way back to my bedroom, I tripped and nearly tumbled down the impossibly steep stairs. I was thinking about Susannah, and how Ms. Parker had nothing on me when it came to stress and back pain. So it wasn't until I'd crawled back into bed that I remembered two other people hadn't turned out in response to Linda's arachnophobic screams.

# Chapter Nine

Hardly more than an hour had passed when I was partially awakened by a loud pounding noise.

"Be still, my heart," I murmured, and turned over to go back to sleep. It wasn't my fault, and therefore not a sin, that I had been dreaming about the not-unattractive Billy Dee Grizzle.

The pounding persisted, and eventually it became clear to my sleep-deprived brain that someone was banging on the door and shouting. In my dreams, Billy Dee had only grunted.

I flung on my modest terry robe and staggered to the door. When I opened it, Joel Teitlebaum nearly knocked me over.

"There's a dead woman on the stairs!" he shouted.

"Grannie Yoder?" I cried happily. Not that I was glad the old woman was haunting the place again, but I was relieved finally to have a confirmation of my sightings. Ever since the first time I saw Grannie Yoder's ghost, Susannah has accused me of being as loony as a lake in Maine. The nerve of that girl!

"Whatever her name is, there's a dead woman on the stairs," repeated Joel. He was still very agitated, and his eyes looked as if they just might pop out of his face.

I grabbed one of his flailing arms. "Calm down, dear. It's only the ghost of my dear, departed grandma. She was far more dangerous in life, believe you me."

Joel wrenched his arm from my restraining grip. "This is *not* a ghost, Miss Yoder! This is a real live woman! Uh, I mean a real dead woman."

I must have flung Joel's spindly frame out of the way, because the next thing I knew I was at the bottom of our impossibly steep stairs. Sure enough, in a heap, not unlike a burlap bag of potatoes, lay the crumpled form of Miss Brown. Not even the Chinese acrobats I'd seen at the circus in Somerset could assume a position like this. I leaned over for a closer look, but I didn't touch her. Mama had made us kiss Grannie Yoder after she was dead, and I'd had nightmares afterward for weeks.

"Are you sure she's dead?"

Joel nodded. "She's still slightly warm, but I can't find a pulse anywhere. Who the hell is she?"

I felt a stabbing pain run through my gut. Sheer terror, I'm sure. "One of my guests. She checked in early yesterday, and then I never saw her again."

"Better call the police," said Joel, who had calmed down significantly. "And, I suppose, an ambulance. Just to be on the safe side."

I called both. At the risk of making myself seem like I have a heart made out of dumplings, I will admit that at this point I was hoping not only that Miss Brown was dead, but that all her relatives were dead as well. What with those stairs being so steep, I was clearly liable. To settle a suit of this magnitude, not only would I have to sell off the PennDutch, but Susannah and I would be indentured servants for the rest of our lives. Even that obnoxious little Shnookums would have to be pawed off for a few pennies. Come to think of it, even the darkest clouds have silver linings.

Jeff Myers is our Chief of Police, and as nice a man as you could hope to meet. We were in grade school together, and he was the one boy whom I didn't mind spitting paper wads at me. Of course he's married now. Anyway, he showed up in no time flat and handled everything as smoothly as Freni does her shoofly pie dough. In less than an hour he had Miss Brown shipped off to the county morgue, for she was indeed dead. And in that time he had managed to interview everyone in the Inn, except for myself. That he did over a cup of coffee in the kitchen.

"May as well," he said, when I offered it to him. "We were planning to leave on vacation in three hours anyway. No use trying to hit the sack now. I'll just let Tammy do the driving."

"Where are you off to?" I asked. Tammy Myers, his wife, is a nice-enough woman, but dingier than a mailbox on a gravel road. They have three children, Sarah, David, and Dafna, who are almost grown. That the woman never misplaced them when they were infants is nothing short of a miracle. If his wife was going to do the driving while Jeff slept, somebody sane needed to know their destination.

"We're going to Niagara Falls," said Jeff, "then camping up

in Canada for two weeks. I'll be leaving my assistant in charge."

"Keep her away from the edge," I advised sagely.

"What?"

"Nothing."

"Now, Mags, about this Brown woman, you say you never saw her again after you showed her to her room? Until Mr. Teitlebaum found her, I mean."

"That's right. I didn't see a sign of her. Of course, she wasn't easy to see, if you know what I mean."

"Uh-huh. Apparently none of the other guests saw or heard her either, at least not while she was alive. Neither did anyone hear a scream when she fell down the stairs, although one man, let's see," he briefly consulted his notes, "a Mr. Grizzle, said he thought he heard a thump. Of course, that might have been Mr. Teitlebaum pounding on your door."

"Probably. And what about Joel Teitlebaum? What was he doing up, anyway? I mean, he seems like a nice kid and all, but shouldn't he have a bedtime?" Mama had made me go to bed by nine every night until the day she died.

Chief of Police Myers glanced at his notes again. "Mr. Teitlebaum claims to have been in your parlor, deeply engrossed in one of your books. Something about Amish rabbis I think. Anyway, according to him, after that spider incident with young Linda McMahon, he couldn't get back to sleep, so he went back down to the parlor. He heard a thump also, but no scream. He said he read another paragraph or two of that damned book—oh, sorry, Mags—before he got up to investigate."

"Maybe she was too drunk to scream," I suggested hopefully. If it was a drunk who fell down your stairs, even though they were impossibly steep, didn't that absolve you of at least some of the liability?

"Maybe," said Chief Myers, "but personally I don't think that's the case. Drunks seldom hurt themselves when they fall. All that booze makes them too flexible. Read about this guy out in San Francisco who fell seventeen stories down an empty elevator shaft. Dead drunk, of course. Hardly got hurt at all."

Suddenly I remembered why I didn't like Jeff so much. He had an annoying habit of always letting logic get in the way. "Well, okay, what if she wasn't drunk then, and somebody pushed her. Then it still wouldn't be my fault, would it?"

Chief Myers's sinfully blue eyes danced in amusement. "You would rather it was murder than face a lawsuit?"

I tried to swallow a huge lump that had somehow lodged in my throat. Perhaps Freni's dumplings weren't as fluffy as I had always believed. "Murder? Who said anything about murder?"

Jeff Myers chuckled. "Ah, you mean it might have been only a friendly sort of push?"

It was time to retreat, and fast. A verdict of murder, it seemed then, would be just as ruinous to the Inn as a lawsuit. "Maybe she fell while sleepwalking, or maybe she decided to come downstairs without turning the hall light on first."

"Maybe," said the Chief. "Then again, maybe not. I think your murder theory has its points."

"My theory?" You see how things always get twisted around, then put back on me? "And what points are those?"

The Chief yawned. "I shouldn't be telling you any of this

stuff, but what the hell. This Miss Brown took a pretty bad fall, but it wasn't the fall that put those marks on her face."

"What marks?" I hadn't seen any marks. Then again, I hadn't looked at her face all that closely. It might have been Yasir Arafat lying there, for all I really knew.

"Marks," said the Chief tiredly. "Kind of like bruises. Fresh bruises that haven't had a chance to darken. Sort of in a fingerprint pattern."

I swallowed another one of Freni's dumplings. "She might have had those marks before she even checked in," I pointed out hastily. "She might have been covering them up with makeup, and then taken it off when she went to bed. Most women take off their makeup at night, you know." At least I assumed they did. I never wore any makeup, and as for Susannah, if she took off her makeup at this point, her face might shatter.

"Maybe, maybe, maybe," said the Chief. He yawned again, in spite of my coffee. "But whatever the reason for those marks, we're not going to find out tonight. Nor are we going to find out why or how she fell. We're just going to have to wait out the coroner's report. In the meantime, I'm having that room sealed off. Might still be a clue or two in there we'll need if this turns out to be foul play. Now, I've got a couple of big pike up in Canada with my name on them, so I'm outta here. Don't worry, Mags, my Assistant Chief is as good as they come." He stood up and stretched—a most immodest act on his part. "If there is any sort of legal trouble, you can always give Alvin a call."

"Not as long as Chip and Dale are around," I said. Alvin Hostetler, another distant cousin, must have attended law school somewhere on the Great Barrier Reef off Australia. His nickname around these parts is Jaws, and it was his mother who bestowed it on him after he took her to court to sue for back allowance. He was eighteen at the time. The case was thrown out of court, of course, but it gives you an idea of Alvin's character. I would sooner dance naked on Hernia's main street than do business with a shark like that. Still, if it did come down to losing the PennDutch, I might have to give in to rubbing fins with Alvin.

Chief Myers bid me a sleepy good night. Before I went back to bed I searched our spidery cellar for the bottle of brandy I knew was hidden there. "For snakebite," Papa told me once. We have very few poisonous snakes in Pennsylvania, but Papa, who was outdoors a lot, always believed in being prepared. Once or twice a month, unbeknownst to anyone but me, Papa would force himself to go down into the cellar and practice sipping that horrible-tasting brandy, so that if the time ever came when he was bitten by a snake, he'd be able to drink enough to withstand the pain. I found Papa's bottle, or one of its descendants, and, after brushing the cobwebs off, tried a swig myself. Of course it tasted awful. But I braved it out, like Papa, and after a couple more swigs I adjusted to the taste. I felt much more inclined to sleep after that.

I am usually a light sleeper, but even I didn't awaken when the alarm went off at five. Shnookums must have, however, because when I did awaken fifteen minutes later, there he was, lying on my chest, just inches from my face.

"Get that damned dog off me!" I yelled. I know, you probably count that as swearing, but it wasn't. It was simply a statement of fact.

Susannah remained immobile, like a hog in a mud wallow on a hot day.

"Get it off!" I yelled again. Just so you know, I can yell at that dog all I want, and it won't even blink a beady little rat's eye, but if I so much as touch it with my little finger, I have Cujo to contend with.

"Susannah Elizabeth Yoder Entwhistle!"

Still no response from Susannah. The mutt, however, inched up my chest until its tiny mouth filled with little rodent teeth was close enough for me to feel its breath on my face. Except for Papa, no male had ever been so intimate. But it was one thing for Papa to kiss me on the cheek, but quite another for two pounds of hair to insinuate themselves into my space.

Recklessly I poked the critter with my right forefinger. Not viciously, you understand, but just enough to prod him off.

Instantly, all thirty-two ounces of ill-tempered shag sprang to life, and I had a snarling, scrabbling, snapping Shnookums on my hands. Literally. The mangy little mongoose managed to mangle my forefinger in his minuscule mouth, and then, just to be spiteful, piddled on my palm.

That did it! I scooped up the mutt, despite my damaged digits, and tossed him totally off the bed. I'm positive that the fling did not inflict any permanent injury, but to hear the mutt's side of it, you would have thought I'd tried to kill him. He yipped and yapped in that pitiful way wounded canines have of expressing their pain, but in this case the dog out and out lied.

Of course the fact that her dog was only crying wolf was lost on Susannah. At the first pitiful yip she sat bolt upright in bed, like Lazarus reviving from the dead. By his second yip she was wide awake and ready to do battle to protect her offspring. "What have you done to him?" she roared at me. Then she turned to her precious pet and her voice dripped sugar, like a lollipop suspended from a heat lamp. "Oooh, is Mommy's itsy-bitsy shnoogy Shnookums okay? Yes? Is we'ums okay?"

I got up and dressed quickly. I'll say this much for Susan-nah. She has the ability to make getting up at five in the morning on a cold, autumn day preferable to remaining in my warm comfortable bed. There has got to be talent there some-where.

Needless to say, I was not in a chipper mood as I clumped about the kitchen getting breakfast for the Ream party. I made no effort to keep down the racket. That the pots and pans seemed to hurl themselves at the stove, and that my bedroom, with Susannah gone back to sleep in it, was right next door were, however, coincidental.

I had just plopped the platter of eggs and bacon on the table when the Reams showed up. On the dot, just like I knew they'd be. People of their ilk are as tight with their time as they are with their money.

"Uhmm, it smells delicious," said Lydia, who led the way. She was dressed in brand-new designer jeans, a new red flannel shirt, never-before-worn lace-up boots, and a new billed cap that sported a political saying. She looked about as much like the hunters I knew as Freni did.

"Coffee with muscle is in the big pot, decaf in the little, and there's hot water in case anyone wants tea," I said per-functorily.

"Coffee better be strong," growled the Congressman. "Damned impossible to get any sleep around here. First that young bimbo goes into histrionics, then some mystery guest takes a header down those wicked stairs of yours. I can hardly wait to see what you've got planned for tonight."

"There is a banister," I pointed out quickly. "And it's fastened to the wall quite securely. The stairs are really very safe."

"And charming, too," said Lydia graciously. "Very Old World in style. They remind me of Europe."

I flashed her a grateful smile. "Thank you."

"Better do something with those damned stairs," snarled the Congressman.

"Is that a hint?" I asked sweetly. If he's not looking, a woman can push a man down a flight of stairs, just as easily as the other way around.

The three of them sat down and began to eat. I stole another glance at Delbert, and then at the Congressman. They both seemed half-asleep. Like Lydia, they were wearing brand-new duds. Why on earth, I wondered, would anybody wear new clothes to tramp around in a woods, unless they planned to be seen? Granted, these were not your typical interview clothes, but they had to be a long way from comfortable.

"Everything all right, folks?" I asked. Perhaps I was just a wee bit brusque because no one, not even the Congressman, responded right away. Like the obedient child I used to be, they ate in silence.

"Got any more of that delicious apple butter you served last night?" asked Delbert after a while.

"Coming right up."

"Any more of that nice, crisp bacon?" asked the Congressman, suddenly coming to life. For a second I was flattered, but then he added, "Or were those charcoal briquettes?"

"He's only kidding, aren't you, dear?" said Lydia quickly. Her face had colored to the point that it almost matched her shirt. Frankly, I felt more sorry for her than I did angry at the Congressman. I got paid to put up with his rudeness. She, on the other hand, paid his bills. At least that's what the papers said.

"The hell I am," he snapped. "The food here is garbage. The service stinks. The—"

Lydia clamped a dainty, manicured hand over her husband's mouth. She couldn't have been more foolish had she tried to muzzle Shnookums. The Congressman may not have been in the habit of biting, but he showed no hesitation when it came to hitting. The blow he gave her was on the side of the head and with the palm of his hand. It was hard enough so that she tipped back in her chair and had to struggle to regain her balance. Why he simply didn't push her hand away, was beyond me. Papa had never hit Mama to my knowledge, nor she him, and neither of them would so much as raise their voice in front of strangers, no matter how vexed they got.

"What the hell!" said Delbert, jumping up, but beyond that he made no move to intervene.

"Stay out of this," growled the Congressman. "This is a family matter." He stood up himself and grabbed his wife by the arm. "Bring the car around in half an hour," he said, presumably to Delbert, then he dragged his wife out of the room.

Delbert sat mutely down.

Not knowing what else to do, I scurried into the kitchen and got the apple butter. When I returned, Delbert was sitting just as I'd left him.

"Does he do that often?" I asked, setting the apple butter down in front of him.

Delbert appeared to shake himself mentally, and offered me a weak smile. "Of course not."

I leaned forward in my best conspiratorial stance. "I don't vote," I whispered. God forgives unselfish lies. "And I can keep my trap shut tighter than a cork on a jug of raw cider." Oh the shame of having read so many dime novels as a child.

"If he lays a hand on her one more time, I'll kill him."

"Poor woman."

"The man's a bastard. She doesn't deserve any of it."

"Why does she put up with it?"

He shook his head. "Damned if I know. She doesn't need him. It's him who needs her. Her money, her connections. He's just small potatoes politically, and will always be without her support."

"Maybe it's love?" Love had never even managed to sweep me off my feet, much less moved me to accept being boxed up the side of the head.

"Love? Ha! Try pity."

Even that was hard for me to understand. "Maybe you're right. But why do you put up with him? Aren't there other Congressmen you could work for? Or, why not just run for office yourself?"

Delbert stirred the apple butter, like a witch stirring her pot. "There are many mysteries in this world, aren't there, Miss Yoder?"

"The English are full of mysteries," said Freni.

I nearly jumped out of my shoes. "Where in tarnation did you come from?"

"I work here, remember?"

"I thought you quit."

"So, I un-quit. You want a cook for breakfast, don't you?"

I wasn't so sure. Now that the meat-eaters had eaten, and the veggie-devourers were about to descend, Freni might be more of a liability than an asset. "Why don't you cook breakfast for Mr. Grizzle when he comes down," I suggested, "and I'll handle those other picky eaters."

Freni folded her stubby arms over her crisp, starched apron and glared. "Magdalena, I am not the fool you take me for. I've got brains. I can tell when it's time to make a few changes. And I'm not such an old dog that I can't learn new tricks. If it's raw carrots those English want for breakfast, then that's what I'll give them."

If I'd had any brains of my own, I would have come up with a good excuse and sent Freni home with pay. At least just for the next few days. But, alas, at times I can be stupider than Melvin Stoltzfus, who tried to milk a bull and got kicked in the head for his efforts. Mercifully, Melvin was thereafter never fully conscious of his blunder. If only I could be so lucky.

"Just kick me in the head," I said to Freni, "and start cooking."

"What?"

"I think I'll leave you two ladies to your work and check in on the Congressman," said Delbert politely. He was obviously a man who had been well brought up and knew when to be discreet.

After he'd gone, I began to clear off the table, but Freni didn't budge.

"Well," I said at last, "isn't it time to start frying some

eggless, milkless, buckwheat pancakes—in vegetable oil, of course?"

"Not until you apologize."

"For what?"

"For firing me, that's what!"

"I didn't fire you, dear. You quit!"

"You should still apologize, Magdalena Yoder. Your mama would never have treated me this way."

That did it. Even after ten years, just the mention of Mama or Papa has a powerful effect on me. Freni knew this and was playing dirty. What she didn't know was that I had been awakened in the wee hours by a screaming arachnophobiac and had been mangled by a midget mutt. Throw in a crumpled corpse, and I had a full plate. I was in no mood for one of her guilt trips.

"Okay, Freni. Since you 'un-quit,' I'll 'un-apologize.' "

I think Freni also has a Stoltzfus up her family tree. "Apology accepted. Shall I serve butter with the pancakes?"

"Just put it on a plate for those who want it. Mr. Grizzle, however, gets bacon with his."

Freni was remarkably cooperative that morning, and I confess to being lulled into a false sense of complacency. I didn't even get my feathers ruffled when Jeanette Parker came bustling in and demanded to know if the hunting party had left yet.

"I don't know," I said honestly.

"Did they eat?"

I studied her calmly. She was wearing a loose, pajama-like outfit that looked as if it were made from burlap sacking. A matching strip of the coarse brown fiber was tied around her

head like a scarf, and knotted on top. The two ends stood
almost straight up and looked for all the world like deer ears.
Almost none of her carrot-red hair was showing.

"What color is your coat?" Too much had happened for me
to remember it from the day before.

"What?"

"Your coat. Is it at least red or blue?"

"My coat is none of your damned business, Ms. Yoder!"

"Suit yourself." Even Mama would have lost patience with
this woman.

"Well, have they eaten or not?" She was tapping away
impatiently with a brown brogan. A flamenco dancer she was
not.

"I don't divulge my guests' activities. Even yours."

"What's that supposed to mean?"

I didn't know. But now I wished I did. For a brief moment
Jeanette looked like the cat who had been caught with her
paw in a fishbowl.

"Orange or tomato juice?" I asked as pleasantly as I could.

Just then Freni entered with a stack of buckwheat pancakes and a jug of warm, homemade maple syrup. Just before
she sat down, I could see Jeanette's brown, burlap-covered
chest inhale the aroma that was wafting from the plate.

"Any more for me?"

I turned to see Billy Dee Grizzle standing in the doorway.
The dark circles under his eyes made him look older than I
had remembered. Much too old for Susannah, for sure. And
there seemed to be a bruise or a scratch on his right cheek-
bone that I hadn't noticed before. Perhaps he had whacked
himself with the shovel while digging for night crawlers. That
sort of thing happens, you know. Myrna Stoltzfus, who was my

best friend in grammar school, once knocked herself out with her own lunch pail.

"There's plenty more," I said. "Do you want coffee?"

"Caffeine has been shown to cause cancer in laboratory rats," said Jeanette, her mouth already full of pancake.

Billy laughed. "So has too much sex."

"What?"

Billy ignored her and sat down. "I'd love some coffee, Miss Yoder."

"Magdalena," I mouthed.

As I was pouring his coffee, Joel and Linda came into the room. "Have they left yet?" they both asked at once.

"That's what I want to know," said Jeanette. Her mouth was again full of pancake, and little pieces sprayed out when she talked.

"Well, come on, guys, we gotta find out," exhorted Linda. She, for one, seemed pretty chipper. It was certainly not obvious that she had recently suffered a near death experience at the hands of something with eight feet.

"Relax, folks," drawled Billy Dee. "Garrett's Buick pulled out of here about twenty minutes ago. They're long gone."

Jeanette brayed and sprayed something unprintable, and then shoved in another bite.

"Well, we can still catch up with them, can't we?" asked Joel. Judiciously, he chose to sit as far as he could from Jeanette. Linda sat down beside Billy.

"It's worth a try," said Jeanette, showing me more pancake than I cared to see. "Even a forest filled with hunters is bound to be safer than this dump. I say we hit the road, and pronto."

"A state forest is an awfully big place," said Linda. I examined her face for signs of Stoltzfus blood.

"It doesn't matter a hill of beans," explained Billy Dee patiently. "We want to catch them coming out with their buck, not just tramping around in some dang woods. We want a picture the reporters can sink their teeth into."

I swallowed hard. "Reporters?"

"At the woods," Billy reassured me, "when they come back to the car. Not here, Miss Yoder."

"But what about their poor deer?" Linda cried.

Billy patted her shoulder.

"Don't worry," I hastened to reassure her, "hundreds of other deer will be killed as well." Come to think of it, great-grandmother Kauffman was originally a Stoltzfus.

Even Linda surprised me then, by bursting into tears and burying her head in Billy's brawny shoulder.

Jeanette glared, but I couldn't tell if it was at me or at Billy, who was sitting opposite me. Then her mouth flew open and the remnants of at least half of a buckwheat pancake came spewing out.

"Gross," said Billy Dee, who is otherwise so polite.

"Eggs!" she rasped.

"What?" I demanded. I was in no mood for false accusations.

"There's an eggshell in the pancakes. So there's got to be eggs!"

"Prove it."

Jeanette poked around in the detritus on her plate and eventually came up with a little white speck that shouldn't have been worth mentioning. "There!"

"Freni!"

Freni materialized almost immediately, wiping her hands on her apron. "Yes?"

"Freni, did you put eggs in those pancakes?"

Freni looked me straight in the eye. "Didn't the children of Israel put straw in their bricks?"

"What?"

"She's nuts," Jeanette had the nerve to say.

"Freni, you weren't making bricks, you were making pancakes. Did you use eggs?"

Freni crossed her arms over her ample, apron-covered bosom and stamped her right foot three times. Except for the arm-crossing, I've seen bulls act just like that before they charge.

"Well, Freni?"

"You cook for the crazy English, Magdalena. I quit!"

"Please, God," I prayed, "let her stay quit until this crowd of English has crossed the Red Sea."

Unfortunately God does not always ignore our prayers. I would much rather have had to deal with a continuance of complaints than with a corpse clutching Mama's Dresden Plate quilt.

# Chapter Ten

### FRENI HOSTETLER'S
### BUCKWHEAT PANCAKE RECIPE

$1/2$ cup all-purpose flour
$3/4$ cup buckwheat flour
3 tablespoons sugar
1 teaspoon baking powder
$1/2$ teaspoon salt
Pinch cinnamon
3 eggs
1 cup light cream
2 tablespoons bacon grease

Sift together dry ingredients. Hand-beat eggs and cream, just until blended. Add bacon grease to liquid. Stir well. By stages pour and stir liquid ingredients into dry mixture until it is smooth and of batter consistency.

Pour or spoon batter onto a hot, cast-iron griddle that has been liberally greased with lard. Fry until upper surfaces of pancakes are pocked with bubbles. Turn and fry until reverse side is golden brown.

Serve oozing with fresh butter and dripping with maple syrup. Homemade pork and sage sausages are the perfect complement.

# Chapter Eleven

I took over in the kitchen. I stirred together some water, some vegetable oil, some all-purpose flour, some buckwheat flour, and some baking powder. I left out the salt and the sugar because both Jeanette and Linda informed me that they were worse than poison, and Jeanette threatened to sue me if these impurities ever passed her lips again on my premises. The pinch of cinnamon I just plain forgot.

I fried the mixture on a different griddle that had been sparsely coated with vegetable oil. The pancakes, if that is what you wish to call them, were flat, heavy, miserable things that broke apart when I turned them. They had all the aroma and appeal of week-old cow-pies, but most of the guests loved them.

"I don't mean to offend you, Miss Yoder," said the ever polite Billy Dee, "but I don't suppose there are any of Mrs. Hostetler's pancakes left back in the kitchen?"

Jeanette glared openly at him, and Linda unsuccessfully tried to suppress a shudder. I trotted back to the kitchen and piled up a plate of all Freni's pancakes that I wasn't capable of eating myself. When I placed it in front of Billy Dee his face lit up like a kerosene lamp with a freshly cleaned globe. "Any bacon back there?" he asked hopefully.

Of course I didn't disappoint Billy Dee. I retrieved a plate of home-cured bacon, fried crisp but not crumbly, and placed it proudly in front of him. Billy Dee was obviously delighted, but the other three reacted like I do when someone lights up a cigarette in my presence. Actually, they were probably more polite. They simply retreated to the far end of the table and huddled together in a defensive posture undoubtedly intended to ward off meat molecules that might break loose from Billy's bacon and bombard them. For the remainder of their scant meal they remained in their closed cluster and conversed in hushed, conspiratorial tones.

That was just fine with me. I loaded up a plate for myself and joined the more convivial carnivore.

"Isn't meat-eating inconsistent with your stand on hunting?" I asked him pleasantly.

Billy Dee bit into another slice of bacon. "Not at all, Miss Yoder. In the animal kingdom there've always been, and will always be, carnivores. They kill, and then eat what they kill. You know, like lions and leopards and things.

"And then there's the scavengers, like the jackals. They eat the meat the carnivores leave behind. Think of me as a scavenger. Someone else killed this pig and left it behind. I'm simply cleaning up after him."

"As can be expected, your analogy holds up only so far," I

was bold enough to say. "I mean, if it's all right for lions and leopards to kill for meat, why isn't it all right for Congressman Ream and his party?"

Billy Dee smiled patiently at me. "Lions and leopards are biologically programmed to kill other animals. They do it for survival. They don't have no choice. The Congressman does."

"Ah, but the jackals are just like the lions, aren't they? They're programmed to scavenge meat. They don't have any choice either. But you do!"

Billy defiantly stuck another slice of bacon into his grinning mouth. "Think of my scavenging as a service to you and the rest of mankind. Whatever bacon I eat, there's less for you to have to worry about. I am unselfishly defiling my body so that you can lead a cleaner, purer life. I'm doing the right thing. The morally correct thing."

"Maybe, but you don't sound very politically correct."

He laughed heartily. "Billy Dee Grizzle is definitely not politically correct."

"How, I mean why, did you change your mind about hunting?" I asked him. "I overheard you telling the Congressman last night that you, yourself, used to hunt."

He seemed genuinely surprised at my question. "Don't you read the papers?"

I must have blushed with embarrassment. As much as I love to read, I am too cheap to have either the Harrisburg or Pittsburgh papers delivered. As for the little weekly rag published in Hernia, its lead story that week concerned a rash of ulcerated udders on Amos Troyer's dairy farm.

Billy Dee was too polite to let me squirm in my ignorance. "It happened almost exactly four years ago," he explained quickly. "We'd just moved up here from Texas. I was deer hunting." His eyes left my face and seemed to focus on the quilting frame across the room. "I had my daughter with me. Jennifer Mae. She was eleven years old." He paused.

"Jennifer is a pretty name," I said to encourage him.

He nodded. "She was my only kid. Her mama died when she was just seven. Anyway, Jenny Mae got tired of hunting and wanted to go back and rest in the pickup. I let her." He swallowed. "It weren't all that far. The pickup, I mean. She would've been all right, except that she got kinda turned around."

"I understand."

"No, you don't. Jenny Mae never made it back to that damned truck. She was wearing this white bow in her hair, like the one her mama used to put in for her. I didn't have the heart to tell her not to wear it. I didn't think there was a need for it, really. She was with me the whole time, except for then, and I was wearing an orange vest."

He paused again, and this time, dreading what he was about to say, I did not encourage him further.

He went on anyway. "It was me, her own daddy, who mistook that bow for a white tail. It was me that shot my own little girl off this earth."

I expected him to break down and sob, but he didn't. "Not that it mattered in comparison to Jenny Mae's death, but it woulda been ruled an accident if it hadn't been for them folks over there."

"Jeanette, Joel, and Linda?"

"Especially her." I just knew he meant Jeanette. "I still don't know how, but immediately they were all over the place like smoked-out hornets. They had the press with them and before I could catch my breath I was charged with involuntary manslaughter. I didn't stand no chance in court."

I gave him a chance to catch his breath and waited quietly until he resumed his tale.

"I got sent up for three years. I know it ain't much, and I probably even deserved it. But the thing is, Miss Yoder, they made out like I'd almost intended to kill Jenny Mae."

"They actually said that?"

"No, not in so many words. But that's what it came down to. They made me out to be some mean, horrible monster who didn't care about what happened to his little girl. They said that by taking her along with me, I was not only choosing to break the law, but I'd publicly given up all rights to be her father."

He rubbed the corners of his eyes with the palm of his hand, although I could see no tears. "I think the worst thing is that they didn't give me no time to react or mourn her death. I was in shock, Miss Yoder. I was absolutely stunned. I just couldn't believe what had happened. And then they were on me. That's what I mean by not being able to catch my breath."

"I see."

"I don't even remember her funeral, Miss Yoder. I can't even say for sure if I was there. Miss Yoder, Jeanette and them other two robbed me of my daughter's death." He made a dismissing motion with his right hand. "Of course I can't expect you to understand that."

"But I do understand." I really did. When Mama and Papa were killed in that horrible accident, I wanted to mourn for them with every fiber of my being. I wanted to feel the pain completely, for as long as I needed to, before having to learn how to cope with it and get on with my life. But of course I didn't have the luxury of orchestrating my own emotional recovery, not with a burden like Susannah to deal with. Following our parents' death, Susannah acted out so completely that ninety-nine percent of my energy was diverted to her and her recovery. Susannah was still a long way from recovery, and I had yet to mourn. Of course, I wasn't about to tell Billy Dee all that. We Swiss do not readily share our emotions, and certainly not with comparative strangers.

Still, Billy Dee seemed to appreciate my saying that I understood, even if he didn't necessarily believe it. He reached out and patted my hand. Needless to say, this embarrassed me terribly, and I reacted as I normally do when I'm embarrassed —by talking.

"I do understand about the mourning part," I assured him. "What I don't understand is why you've turned around and joined them. Isn't that carrying the 'turn the other cheek' principle just a little too far?"

He leaned halfway over the table and lowered his voice to a whisper. "I haven't joined them, Miss Yoder, I've infiltrated them."

"You what?"

"Well, true, I have given up hunting. I can't bring myself to touch a gun no more, not after Jenny Mae's death. But I ain't anti-hunting, like they are. I still think responsible people should have the right to hunt. It's just that I wasn't responsible."

"But if you don't believe in their cause, why are you with them?"

He whispered even softer. "Because I want to keep them

from doing to other people what they did to me. I'm here to keep tabs on them, Miss Yoder. To keep their fanaticism in line."

"And they don't suspect you?" Jeanette might be obnoxious, but she surely wasn't stupid.

"I suppose they do. Still, I think they're glad to have me. I suspect they're kinda proud of having a convert in their ranks. It shows others that if I can see the way, surely they can too. I'm a walking testimony to the rightness of their position. Whether or not I'm really sincere is something they prefer not to think about."

"Unless, of course, you choose to pig out on bacon right under their noses."

We burst out laughing, and then almost immediately contained ourselves. The three down at the other end of the table were looking in our direction, and they did not appear to be at all amused.

"What's so damned funny?" demanded Jeanette, but she didn't seem to want an answer. "I should think that with a major lawsuit hanging over your head, Miss Yoder, you wouldn't have time to be so frivolous. I should think that your agenda for the day would include finding a good lawyer and a carpenter. Why, I nearly tripped coming down those stairs myself."

"There is a banister!" I almost screamed. It would almost be worth a lawsuit, however, to see Jeanette take a tumble. Then again, the damage incurred to my stairs would offset any satisfaction.

Billy Dee reached forward and patted my hand. "Don't you go worrying none, Miss Yoder. There ain't gonna be no lawsuit. And even if there is, you ain't gonna lose. Why heck, those stairs ain't so steep. Friend of my in Dallas fell down a much steeper stairs, only he didn't die, and it still took the jury three days to come to a decision."

"What did they decide?" I held my breath.

"The plaintiff won, of course. But like I said, they were much steeper stairs."

"How much did the plaintiff win?" I was going to have to stop throwing out those notices from Publishers Clearing House.

"Hardly anything. Only about three and a half mill, I think."

For a brief and unforgivable second, I hated Mama and Papa. If they hadn't gotten themselves creamed between a milk tanker and a load of shoes, I wouldn't be in such a pickle. Since I was sinning anyway, I vowed never to drink another glass of milk and to go barefoot whenever possible.

"Hey, shouldn't we be heading out to the woods?" asked Joel, breaking into my reverie. For a fanatic, he seemed to be remarkably moderating.

Everyone agreed, including myself, that it was long past time they hit the road. I surprised them by dashing into the kitchen and returning with sack lunches. "They're all the same," I said pointedly. "Oatmeal batter bread sandwiches with strawberry preserves, and peanut butter cookies."

"Better not be any eggs in here," growled Jeanette.

"Did you use organic peanut butter in the cookies?" asked Linda.

I smiled benevolently. "Of course, dear." I wasn't lying, either. I'd checked my dictionary before going to bed the night before. According to Webster, organic things were those that were, or had been, alive and that contained carbon. Even the off-brand of peanut butter I bought used peanuts that had once been alive and contained carbon. Of course, it is quite possible that Linda meant to ask if the peanuts had been grown by the aid of organic fertilizers and without pesticides. But that's not what she said, was it? So, in the words of Susannah, "Tough cookies."

Speaking of Susannah, I hadn't even had a chance to sit down again after the others left, when she came billowing into the room. Everything billows about Susannah, except for her bosom, which is even smaller than mine, and barely capable of bobbing, much less billowing.

We grunted our greetings. That's more than can be said for most sisters who don't get along and have good reason for feeling crabby when they meet. My crabbiness was understandable, of course. As to the origin of Susannah's, I didn't have a clue.

"Get up on the wrong side of my bed?"

Susannah sat down and began picking at the remains of Billy Dee's breakfast. "I wouldn't have gotten up at all if the idiots above me had kept the noise down."

"What do you mean?" The idiot above my bedroom happened to be Garrett Ream.

Susannah, the true scavenger, sucked at a strip of Billy Dee's half-eaten bacon. "What I mean," she said irritably, "is that Mr. Big-shot Congressman and his goody-two-shoes, Barbie-doll of a wife were having a knock-down, drag-out fight."

"He hit her?"

"How should I know? I didn't see it. I heard it."

"What did they say?" Contrary to what you may be thinking, I have a right to know what goes on in my establishment.

"What's it to ya, Mags?"

"A fresh stack of pancakes and all the bacon you can suck —I mean, eat."

"Deal." Susannah took Shnookums out of the nether reaches of her billowiness and set him down on Billy Dee's syrupy plate, which he proceeded to lick clean.

"Well?" I asked, after a great deal of patience had expired.

"Well, he accused her of having a thing for that cute aide of his. What's his name?"

"Delbert James."

"Yeah, him. Of course she denied it. But that wasn't the interesting part."

"What was it, then?"

"I'm getting to it! The interesting part was when she said something about him having had an affair with Ms. Bitchy-Pants. You know, the one with the red hair."

"Jeanette Parker?"

"Mags, would you stop interrupting me? Anyway, I nearly fell out of bed laughing when I heard that. I thought I might even have heard wrong, but no, she said it again."

I was sure Susannah had heard wrong. As obnoxious as they both were, I couldn't, by any stretch of the imagination, see the Congressman being attracted to a woman like Jeanette. Not when he had the charming Lydia for a wife. I decided to push my luck with Susannah. "What exactly were her words?" I begged.

"See, you don't believe me!"

At that my baby sister scooped up her sticky-footed stowaway and stashed him back in the nether reaches from whence he'd come.

"I do believe you!" I protested.

"How much?"

I can only be pushed so far. "Enough to not kick you out of my room and make you sleep on the floor in the parlor."

Susannah stuck her tongue out at me but cooperated nonetheless. "Her exact words were: 'You're the one who slept with Jeanette Parker, maybe it's you who should pay the price.' Something very close to that at any rate."

I sat down heavily, like the proverbial ton of bricks. "Anything else interesting?"

Susannah took a minute to coo at Shnookums in his dank and undoubtedly dreary hideaway. "Yeah," she said finally, "Lydia Ream said something about Jeanette being Linda's mother."

"Aha! So they're not, uh, I mean—"

"Lesbian lovers?"

"Susannah!"

"Oh, Mags, you are so provincial. This is the nineties. Why don't you get with the times like I am!"

"You are a wanton woman, Susannah."

"And you're egg drop soup." Susannah laughed heartily at her own little joke. Her bony, braless bosom bobbed up and down like a fishing cork on Miller's pond. From somewhere within the powdered plumage of her cascading costume Shnookums sneezed.

"Bless you."

"Thank you," said Susannah on Shnookums's behalf.

"What's more, Magdalena, you don't even know the half of it. What else I heard will really knock your socks off. It did mine."

"Enlighten me," I begged. Susannah watches "Geraldo" and reads those magazines that describe two-headed aliens mating with farm animals. Nothing short of amputation could separate her from her socks.

"Can I borrow the car this morning if I tell you? I want to go shoe shopping in Somerset."

I cringed at the mention of shoes. "Susannah, don't you think it would be prudent to save your pennies, especially at the moment?"

"What do you mean?"

"I mean . . . because . . . well . . . you know, there might be a lawsuit."

Susannah laughed so hard that I truly feared for Shnookums's life. "You don't honestly believe there is going to be a lawsuit, do you, Mags?" she finally managed to say.

"I most certainly do. I mean, there is a chance."

"Some chance! Mags, you really should watch more TV. They have to prove negligence in a suit. It can't just be because the stairs are steep."

"And there is the banister," I reminded her.

"Exactly. So you see, you don't have a thing to worry about, do you?"

"I sure hope you're right. But I still don't think shopping is such a good idea right now."

"Maybe not for you," said Susannah wickedly. "The Inn is in your name, not mine. Remember?"

"Thanks a lot!" But she had a point. I was the responsible adult. Call me an enabler, but Susannah, despite her burgeoning years, is not capable, much less culpable, which is precisely why Mama and Papa left the Inn to me.

"Come on, Mags, let me have the car," Susannah begged, "and I promise to tell you that juicy bit of information that is guaranteed to knock your socks off."

"Okay," I said at last. The gas tank was almost empty, and Hernia didn't have a full-service station. Since Susannah would rather go to church than pump her own gas, it was a safe bet that she wasn't going to get very far.

"Goody!" cried Susannah. She rubbed her hands gleefully together and then cupped them to her mouth like a little girl about to gossip to her best friend. "Not only is that awful Jeanette Linda's mother," she whispered, "but Congressman Ream is her father."

"Come on!" I'm almost positive I felt at least a tug on my hose.

"I kid you not. And not only that, but I think Jeanette's been blackmailing the Congressman. I think she's been putting the screws on him for years. Her showing up yesterday was no coincidence. And you know what else? I think the Congressman's wife has known about this all along, but for some stupid reason she won't or can't divorce him. That's what I think."

"You think? You think? Susannah, blackmail is a serious crime. You can't be making allegations like that based on things you heard through the ceiling. I can't believe Lydia Ream would put up with such a sordid situation."

"I have news for you, Sis. Lydia Ream is not the saint you make her out to be. I heard her telling her husband that it was his turn to start paying, remember? And she didn't sound like a choir member when she said it either. In fact, she used words that you have probably never even heard of. It's obvious that she's mad as hell about the blackmail and isn't going to take it anymore."

"I think they call that circumstantial evidence."

"You are such a skeptic, Mags. You don't believe anything unless you have pages of documentation."

"I still don't believe Shnookums is a dog. Circumstantial evidence leads me to believe that he is a species of hairy rat."

"That does it!" Susannah stood up in a billowy huff and stormed from the table. At the doorway she stopped. "And one more thing, *Miss* Yoder, Billy Dee Grizzle already has a girlfriend, and Delbert James just happens to be gay!"

"And so is Shnookums!" I screamed at her back. Any animal psychiatrist would have a field day with a canine that was perpetually carried around in a purse or a half-empty bra.

To my disappointment, Susannah didn't respond to my last remark. Shnookums, however, did. I didn't get a chance to see the puddle the nervous little pooch produced, but Susannah bolted for the bathroom, and later on I found that pile of polyester swirls she'd been wearing crammed into my hamper.

# Chapter Twelve

The second my car, with Susannah at the wheel, disappeared from sight, I bolted up the steep stairs of my gloriously empty inn and headed straight for the sealed-off room. It was a little tricky getting the orange tape off the doorjamb in such a way that I could replace it without anyone's being the wiser. Only a sharp-eyed detective would notice my tampering when I was through, and even Chief Myers, God bless him, wasn't that perceptive. If he was, he would undoubtedly have noticed that his wife, Tammy, had knock-knees, a mouth like a mule, and brayed when she laughed. He should have bought her a saddle instead of that engagement ring, back when we were in high school.

I don't know what I expected to find in Miss Brown's room. I simply started looking through her things, which, with the exception of a pair of rinsed-out hose hanging on the towel rack, a pair of brown house slippers with gray piping, and the shoes and dress she'd worn the day before, were all still in her suitcase. Her purse had apparently been taken by the Chief.

That her suitcase was locked didn't slow me down a bit. Every Mennonite girl worth her bonnet knows how to wield a hairpin with the skill of a surgeon. I had that drab little valise open in less time than it takes Freni to smile, not that it did me any good. Two beige bras, two mostly white pairs of panties, a gray sweater, a pair of brown slacks, an oatmeal-colored blouse, and a toothbrush didn't tell me a whole lot more than I already knew—except that she wore a size ten panty, which meant that her dress had done a fine job of disguising her big caboose.

Out of habit I started to make her bed, which had apparently been slept in, but then caught myself. Corpses aren't known for their bed-making skills, especially after they've been carted off to the morgue. Hernia might not have the sharpest police department around, but they weren't complete slouches either. At least that's what I thought back then.

I took one last quick look around. None of my furnishings had disappeared. The cheaply framed print of "The Angelus" still hung on the wall, the Gideon Bible remained on the desk, and in the bathroom I could still see two towels. There were even two drinking glasses on the sink instead of the usual one, which was quite all right with me. Any guest who wanted to leave usable items behind was welcome to do so.

If I must say so myself, I did a superb job of replacing the tape. Only a slight wrinkle on the end of one of the strips betrayed my intrusion, and for all I know, it had already been there.

The next item on my agenda was to call the phone numbers Miss Brown had listed on her guest application. Of course, they were toll calls, but what's a buck or two when you are about to lose your shirt—make that a blouse—to the cleaners?

I called the number listed as her residence first. After about the fourth ring a mechanical voice, supposedly female, got on the line, told me my call could not be completed as dialed, and then proceeded to lecture me on how I should consult my phone directory in the future.

The second call, to her place of business, was slightly more satisfying. That call was answered on the second ring by a rather hearty-sounding male voice. "Jumbo Jim's Fried Chicken and Seafood Palace," it said. "Jim speaking."

"Is this the workplace of Miss Heather Brown?" I asked.

"I'm sorry, but you must have a wrong number," said Jumbo Jim. He had a very pleasant voice, sort of like the Chief's, but with just a tinge of southern twang.

"Is this 410-555-3216?"

"Correcto. And what's your number, doll?"

Of course I was taken aback. "I don't give my number to strangers."

Jumbo Jim laughed, but I didn't feel he was laughing at me. " 'Strangers' is a relative term, doll. Most relatives are strangers. Or at least pretty strange."

"You're telling me!" My double first cousin Agnes Miller married a wealthy corset manufacturer and moved not only to Philadelphia, but to the snobbiest address on the Main Line. When the bottom fell out of the corset market, Agnes had to work at the hat-check stand at the Club just to make ends meet. Her husband got work there as a busboy. Of course, both Agnes and her husband wore disguises to their jobs, and it was fourteen years before the other members discovered that Agnes, the hat-check girl, and Alfred, the busboy, were really their friends and neighbors.

"So, what'll it be, doll?" asked Jim in that wonderful voice.

I'm easily rattled. "One of Hamlet's soliloquies?" I asked hopefully.

Jumbo Jim laughed again. "Sorry, doll, but I sell chicken and shrimp. Did you want to place an order?"

I forced myself to stick with my program. "I'm trying to locate a Miss Heather Brown. This is the number I was given as her place of employment. Are you sure she doesn't work there? Maybe under another name?"

"What does she look like?"

I described Heather to him. The Heather I'd met the day before, of course, *not* the Heather that resembled a bag of potatoes.

"Sorry, doll," said Jim sympathetically. "I know a lot of women like that in Baltimore, but none of them works here."

"In that case, I'm sorry I wasted your time," I said. I knew that mine certainly had not been wasted.

"No problemo, doll. You want to go ahead and place an order anyway? Our special this week is an eight-piece bucket of chicken, extra crisp, and a dozen deep-fried shrimp, all for the low price of $12.99."

"With or without skin?" I asked.

"With, of course. Fat's where it's at. Want that delivered, or are you coming in, hon, to pick it up?"

"I live in Hernia, Pennsylvania, Jim."

"No problemo, doll. Just give me directions from Baltimore. I'm off next weekend. I'll run it up then."

"Just take Interstate 70 all the way up until it joins the Pennsylvania Turnpike. Go west until you get to Bedford.

Then take Route 96 south. I'm at the PennDutch Inn. Everyone in Hernia knows where it is."

"Will do, doll." He hung up.

Of course I was just kidding, but was Jumbo Jim? I could hardly wait until the next weekend to find out. I'm very partial to chicken fried extra crisp.

Having struck out on both phone numbers, and having found nothing of interest in Miss Brown's room, I decided to retire to my own room for a much needed nap. Of course, I tidied up the room a bit and made my bed before lying down on it. Susannah would have thought it stupid to make a bed before you lie on it, but then again, Susannah thinks it's stupid of me to clean the house before I go on a trip. The fact that I wash the breakfast dishes before I go to church on Sunday mornings is, to her, a ridiculous waste of time. Then again, so is church. If cleanliness is next to godliness, as they say, Susannah's best quality is automatically third-rate.

I napped only about twenty minutes. That was just long enough to feel refreshed, and too short to get that groggy, headachy feeling that can result from midday naps. When I got up, I washed my face and put on my sturdiest pair of walking shoes.

From the front closet, next to the check-in desk, I got my winter coat. It is a brown wool hand-me-down that is as old as dirt and as ugly as sin, but I can't bear to part with it. Not only is it as warm as August, but it used to belong to Mama. She would have been wearing it that day she and Papa got run over by the sneaker truck, but Mama was having hot flashes then and chose to leave the coat behind.

Whenever I put on the coat I can still smell Mama on it. I don't mean that Mama smelled bad. And she certainly never wore perfume. She had a slightly musty, earthy smell, not unlike the garden after a rain.

I'd intended to put on my brown and gray plaid scarf, too, but it wasn't on the hook where it should have been. Susannah again. What that woman can't get by begging, she gets by borrowing, but without the owner's permission. At least this time she'd asked me for the car. At any rate, I had to make do with a bright orange strip of polyester that supposedly belonged to Susannah, but which she may well have borrowed from a highway maintenance crew. Thus, decked out warmly, but admittedly not fashionably, I set out the back way for Freni's.

On the back steps I paused to wave at Mose, who happened to be leading Matilda, our main milker, out of the barn. Mose shows up every day, regardless of the weather or his wife's employment situation. I am immensely grateful for this. I hate milking. Even though we own automatic milking machines that you attach directly to the cow's teats, and which do all the work for you, I despise the job. Maybe it's because I wouldn't want something like that attached to me, or maybe it's because I know just how much damage a misplaced cow's hoof can do, but I would rather sell the cows and buy my milk from the store than have to extract it myself. Fortunately, not once following the thirty-six times Freni has quit her job, or the nine times she's been fired, have I had to perform this loathsome chore. Mose, as one of my guests once said, is a "mensch."

Mose and Freni live on their own farm, although actually today the farm is run by their eldest son, John. I suppose that Mose and Freni love their son John, and get along with him reasonably well, but the same cannot be said for their relationship with their son's wife. Barbara Zook was born and raised in one of the western Amish communities, Iowa I think, which is not to disparage them, but I know it's always been an issue. Perhaps it would be less of an issue if Barbara Zook Hostetler was a timid little thing who knew her place in the pecking order.

But this is not the case. To the contrary, Barbara stands at least six feet tall in her woolen hosiery, and is as timid as a Leghorn rooster. Barbara's perceived place in the pecking order is to peck back when pecked. When Freni and Barbara start pecking at each other, more than just feathers fly.

Less than six weeks after John married Barbara, Mose and Freni retired and turned their farm over to their oldest son. That's when Mose came to work for Papa. Then, after Mama and Papa's death, when I started up the PennDutch Inn, Freni jumped at the chance to work for me. She's been jumping at the chance ever since.

There are two ways to get to the farm where Freni and Mose Hostetler live. If you take the road, Augsburger Lane, to the left, and then turn left again on Miller's Run, and then left one more time on Beechy Grove Lane, it's exactly 6.3 miles from the PennDutch. But if you simply go out the back door and head straight out between the old six-seater and the chicken coop, it's only eight tenths of a mile. Even when I have the car I seldom drive it.

The path between the PennDutch and the Hostetler farm is as hard and defined as if it had been poured from concrete. Generations of our two families have used this path, which runs due east and west. Tradition has it that it began as an Indian path and that our common ancestor, Jacob Hochstetler, was taken along this path by the Delaware Indians after he was captured in eastern Pennsylvania in 1750. In fact, when we were growing up, Susannah and I referred to it as "Grandfather's path," as did virtually everyone else we knew.

I could have walked Grandfather's path in the dark or blindfolded and it wouldn't have made any difference. I knew it as well as I knew the varicose veins on my left leg. The path cuts between two fields, now turned over to alfalfa, on our land, and then rises up a low wooded ridge that separates us from the Hostetlers. On the other side of the ridge the path descends and divides two cornfields. It's as simple as that.

I suppose I was day-dreaming as I walked to Freni's that day, but like I said, it didn't really matter. It was too cold for snakes and too warm for ice, although just barely, so I had no need to keep my mind on what my feet were doing. I was free to think about more important things, like, did Billy Dee really have a girlfriend, and was Delbert James really gay, and didn't it bother Susannah that she was probably headed for hell and eternal torment and damnation?

I had just entered the wooded part when a tree to my immediate right seemed to explode, and my face was showered with wood chips. Then I heard a crack like thunder. I dropped to my hands and knees. Forty-three years of living on a farm, even as a pacifist, have taught me what a rifle sounds like.

Almost immediately the rock-hard path in front of me rose up to meet me in a spray of pebble-hard particles. The second crack rang in my ears as I dropped to my stomach and rolled under a clump of evergreen laurel bushes.

"Hey!" I shouted. "This is a person here, not a deer!"

There came no response, either vocal or mechanical. Besides the whining in my ears, the only sound I could hear came from a flock of crows that had been routed from their rookery and were flying off in the general direction of Hernia, com-plaining loudly as they went. When distance finally eliminated their disgruntled caws, the only sound I could hear was the faint cackling of my hens back at the coop. Whoever had shot at me was either not moving, or moving with the stealthy silence of a cat on a hardwood floor. Not a twig cracked, or a fallen leaf rustled.

I lay prone, hidden by the laurel bushes, for the better part of an hour. I don't think fast on my feet, and I'm even slower thinking on my stomach. I had no reason to suspect that who-ever had shot at me was still out there, but no reason to think otherwise. The only sensible thing, it seemed, was to lie there and wait it out. Fortunately, Mama's old wool coat was as warm as Freni's kitchen on baking day.

But how long was long enough? That, of course, I couldn't know for sure, although I did have a fairly accurate barometer of my readiness to make a run for it. About every five minutes or so I tried to rouse myself from my hiding place, and each time my heart pounded so wildly it actually hurt my chest, and my arms and legs would buckle out from underneath me, and I'd fall face down in the leaves again. I probably made more noise trying to see if I could run than I would have if I'd actually run, slapping the bushes with a stick as I went. I don't know why it didn't occur to me that if the hunter really thought I was a deer, or was out to get me personally, he or she could have done so easily within the first five minutes.

Just when I was beginning to gather my wits and strength, and maybe, finally, make a run for it, I heard someone coming down the path. I knew right away it was a someone, and not a something, because he or she was whistling. In Pennsylvania, at least, no critters that walk loud enough to be heard on a hard dirt path are capable of whistling, except for human beings.

I froze in a crouching position and kept my eyes on the path. At first it was impossible to tell if the approaching person was male or female, because both sexes essentially sound alike when they whistle. That's simply because whistling is produced by the mouth alone and has nothing to do with the vocal cords.

Neither could I tell by the footsteps. Perhaps in the days when men routinely weighed more than women, my unsophisticated ear might have been able to detect a difference in tread. Now, however, following the introduction of polyester stretch pants into western culture, it seems to me that women have made significant gains in eradicating this inequality.

Not that the sex of the person approaching was at all germane to my safety. Female fingers are just as capable of pulling gun triggers as male. Probably even more so, since the average woman has a stronger index finger as a result of pushing so many aerosol spray buttons.

But anyway, when the approaching person was still several yards up the path, I could see through the bushes well enough to tell that it was a woman. And an Amish woman at that. I could see clearly the hem of a long blue skirt hanging close to the ground, and a pair of heavy black shoes.

Although the bushes were too thick above me to see anything more, I breathed a huge sigh of relief. The odds of my being shot at by an Amish woman were about the same as the odds of Freni stripping off her clothes and dancing naked on the dining room table for our guests. I said Freni, not Susannah.

Speaking of the devil, the figure was even with me when I

figured out that it was indeed Freni. Freni had broken a shoe-
lace a day or two ago, and I, being out of black, had loaned her
a brown one. Now, there, just inches from my face, a black
lace and a brown lace were striding rhythmically down the
path. Impulsively I reached out of the bushes and grabbed
Freni's left ankle.

I know, that was a terrible thing for me to do. I still can't
believe I did it. It's not like me at all.

Freni not only screamed but did an Olympic-class swivel
and kicked me soundly in the chops with her other foot. Then
she cut loose with a string of potent High German epithets
that would have made her church elders blush, proving once
and for all that pacifism is not necessarily a genetic trait.

I screamed, this time in pain, and stood up in the bushes.
Perhaps it was my screaming as well, or the fact that I somehow materialized, albeit a bit scratched and torn, through the
top of the bush, but Freni screamed even louder. Just like
yawns beget yawns, screams sometimes beget more screams,
and I too found myself screaming louder. There we stood, one
Amish woman on a path, and one Mennonite woman in a
bush, screaming our heads off, and frightening ourselves more
by the second.

Had there been a third person still lurking in the vicinity,
I'm sure it would have been his or her turn to be paralyzed
with fear. Eventually, though, Freni and I got a grip on it, as
Susannah would say, and were merely glaring at each other
when Mose came panting up the path.

"What is it?" he gasped. That, at least, is what he intended
to say. Heavy breathing has a tendency to modify speech.

Freni caught her breath before I could. "Magdalena tried
to scare me to death! She hid in the bushes like a little child

and then grabbed me as I went by." She turned to face me. "Your mama would be so ashamed! Acting like that English daughter of hers." Of course, she meant Susannah.

"I didn't mean to scare you!" I protested. "That's not why I was hiding in the bushes."

Freni blushed, and Mose turned discreetly away while she lectured me. "Magdalena Yoder! At your age? In the bushes like a teenager! Get married first, Magdalena."

I felt myself blush as well. I couldn't believe Freni's assumption—although perhaps I was a bit flattered. "I was in the bushes alone, Freni."

"That is an even greater sin!"

I couldn't help laughing. There I was, being lectured on morality by Freni Hostetler, when less than an hour before someone had tried to kill me. Had they succeeded, I would have died not only a virgin, but having never even been properly kissed. I was indeed flattered by Freni's assumptions.

"Stop that at once," she ordered. "If your mama could see you now, it would break her heart."

"Mama would understand totally." I paused to let Freni gasp. "I was hiding in the bushes because someone was shooting at me."

Freni's mouth clamped shut like a well-oiled mousetrap.

"It's true. I was coming up to see you," I explained, "when someone shot at me with a rifle. See, there?" I pointed to the bullet hole on the tree that overhung the bushes. "And there." I pointed to the ground. "They shot at me twice."

Freni's frown meant she didn't quite believe me but was undecided enough to keep her trap shut for the moment.

"She's telling the truth," Mose said. "I saw Magdalena head on over here, and then a little later I heard two shots, but I thought they were coming from over there." He nodded in the general direction of the state game lands. On days when the wind is right, it sounds like the hunters are right in our own back yard.

"Well, now that we're both here," said Freni without further ado, "I want my job back."

"You what?" I couldn't believe how callous she was.

"My job, Magdalena. You know, where I cook and clean, and do all the things your mama used to do."

"Leave Mama out of this," I said irritably. "I almost got shot in the head. I had to lie hiding in the bushes for an hour —which you just assumed was bundling, or worse even—and you don't have the courtesy to ask how I am?"

Freni looked me quickly up and down. "Except for that scratch on your cheek, and a few twigs on your coat, you look fine, Magdalena."

"Fine? My heart's pounding, my knees are shaking, I look like I've been wrestling with a porcupine, and you say 'fine'?" I clambered angrily out of the bush.

"So maybe you don't look fine after all," said Freni. "You do look, and sound, a little bit crabby. Now, can I have my job back, or what?"

Getting shot at by a stranger, and then being falsely accused of lust in the laurels could make anyone a little bit crabby. But Freni has a way of needling under my skin that not even Susannah can come close to duplicating. There are times when Freni Hostetler and a bad case of chiggers have everything in common. So irritated was I that I forgot I had been on my way to hire Freni back.

"No, you cannot have your job back," I said angrily. "Not

until you apologize for your disgusting accusations, not to mention your lack of general concern."

Mose turned wisely away and headed back down the path.

"In that case, I quit," said Freni.

"You can't quit!" I screamed. "You haven't been re-hired, so you can't quit."

"And not only do I quit," hissed Freni, "but I refuse to come back to work until you apologize for having fired me in the first place!"

"I didn't fire you, Freni. You quit, remember? Or is your memory on its way out too?"

"Your mama would turn over in her grave if she could hear how you speak to me!"

Poor Mama seemed to get more exercise dead than she ever did alive. "Leave Mama out of this," I cried. And then I yielded to temptation. I sank as low as I've ever sunk and will probably ever sink again. "Go back home and boss your daughter-in-law Barbara around. See if you can drive her as crazy as you do me."

I whirled around before I had a chance to look at Freni's face and stomped on down the path after Mose. Mama was undoubtedly spinning like a top, but at the moment I didn't care. Anyway, she had no right to die and leave me in the first place. If Mama hadn't gone and died under a pile of milk-soaked sneakers, Freni Hostetler wouldn't be in my face so much and my life would be that much easier. Feeling thusly cheated, I muttered one of the cuss words I've heard Susannah say and gave Mama an extra spin.

# Chapter Thirteen

Just as I'd thought, Susannah hadn't got very far at all. About a mile down the road the car began to sputter and stall, and half a mile later it quit altogether. Susannah simply left it by the side of the road, walked home, and crawled back into bed. That's where I found her when I got back from my brush with death in the woods.

"Buy out Thom McAn's already?" I asked pleasantly.

Susannah clamped a pillow over her ears. I think Shnookums might have been somewhere inside the pillow case because I heard a faint yelp.

"Go away, Mags. Just leave me alone."

"Where's the car?"

"I didn't even make it past Speicher Creek. You knew it was out of gas, didn't you?"

"Well, I thought you'd at least make it into Hernia."

"Very funny. Now leave me alone!"

It's no fun teasing Susannah when she refuses to fight

back. I settled for telling her about my near-death experience in the woods. Of course she didn't believe me. Her eyes rolled so far back in her head that she would have seen her brain, had there been one to see.

After combing the leaves out of my hair and doctoring my scratches, I cleared off the dining room table and washed all the morning's dishes. Then I went to the tool shed by the barn and got the jerry can of gasoline I keep there for the riding mower.

I am not helpless like Susannah. Maybe it's because I'm older, but Daddy taught me not only how to put gas in the car, but how to change a flat tire. In no time at all the car was purring like a kitten, and I was on my way into Hernia.

Hernia, Pennsylvania, is a nice place to live, but you wouldn't want to visit there. What I mean is, folks who live in and around Hernia are by and large fond of the place and satisfied with their lives. That Hernia lacks commercial and cultural amenities is a plus for them. Visitors, on the other hand, tend to find Hernia boring at best.

The people of Hernia have not capitalized on their Amish and Mennonite neighbors as some other communities have. There are no gift shops selling Pennsylvania Dutch kitsch, and no model farms re-creating authentic Amish life. The PennDutch, I'm proud to say, comes the closest to exploiting this unique heritage, and my operation is small potatoes compared to what I've seen up near Lancaster.

Of course, a lot of English live in Hernia too. Besides the First Mennonite Church on North Elm Street, there are the Methodist and Presbyterian churches, and even a tiny little congregation of devout worshippers out toward the turnpike who call themselves the First and Only True Church of the

One and Only Living God of the Tabernacle of Supreme Holiness and Healing and Keeper of the Consecrated Righteousness of the Eternal Flame of Jehovah.

Susannah and one of her boyfriends attended church there one Sunday just as a joke. They both entered the building on crutches, intending to fake dramatic recoveries during the faith-healing part of the service. Much to everyone's surprise they were healed, at least for a spell, of their penchant for practical jokes.

Four hours after they first entered the tiny cement-block building, they managed to escape with their souls and bodies still intact but their wallets violated. This is the only church I know of that accepts Visa and MasterCard in the offering plate, although it won't accept American Express. At any rate, Susannah's and Chuck's cards were accepted so often that morning, that Susannah had to scrap her plans of buying her own car, and Chuck had to take a second job working out at Miller's Feed Store.

Anyway, besides church, gas, feed, and groceries, there isn't anything in Hernia to spend your money on. Unless you're farming, the odds are Yoder's Corner Market has the corner on your pocketbook.

Samuel Nevin Yoder is my father's first cousin once removed, but I have to pay full price, just like everyone else. Sam's prices are high, I'm told by others who've shopped elsewhere, but since he has no competition, business is usually brisk. Sam's best bargains come in the summertime, when he stocks fresh produce from area farms. His most ridiculous prices, as far as I'm concerned, are for the same items he has brought in from the outside world during the winter months.

Normally I would rather eat fruits and vegetables from

cans than pay the outrageous prices Sam asks for his winter produce. Apparently everyone else in Hernia feels the same, because all Sam's winter produce seems to be permanently limp and wilted. I'm sure I saw the same rubbery head of brown lettuce all season last year, and I half-expected to see it this season as well. I would have recognized it, had it showed up, because last year, after about a month of observing it, I gouged a chunk out of its base with my thumbnail.

Today, despite my principles, and my generally hard-to-open purse, I loaded up my grocery cart with Sam's produce. After a great deal of deliberation—some of it while flat on my face in the woods—I'd come to the conclusion that I might actually hold my expenses down by unloading some of my crisp greens on Sam, in exchange for some of his limp greens. Maybe there was something to the notion that animal protein begets violence in its consumers. After all, I had never seen a violent deer, or even a violent cow, but I'd encountered plenty of snapping dogs. Since just one bite of animal-tinged pancake could turn Jeanette Parker into a howling banshee, threatening to sue, didn't it make sound economical sense to try and placate her with rabbit food? I mean, I have never seen a bunny hopping mad, have you?

Sam seemed to think my idea was a good one. "Because you're buying so much, Magdalena, I'm going to give you a ten percent discount," he said cheerfully.

"Thanks a lot, Sam. Now I can afford that cruise to Hawaii I've been wanting."

Sam smirked. He is genetically incapable of smiling. "Say, I heard that someone took a tumble out at your place last night. A fatal one at that. You give Alvin a call yet?"

My stomach suddenly felt like it was about to fall through

me and hit the floor, and it had nothing to do with the state of Sam's groceries or his prices. "There's a lot of big mouths in this town," I said weakly. "And anyway, it wasn't my fault, Sam. There is a banister she could have hung on to."

Sam smirked again. "Heard some other things too."

"Like what?"

"Like, for instance, Congressman Ream is staying out at your place."

"You've got good ears, Sam. What else have you heard?"

"Nothing much. Just that a bunch of hippy protesters are there as well. Sounds like you have a potential situation on your hands."

"Sam, hippies went out with the sixties. These are just a bunch of concerned citizens." I dug deep into my wallet to find enough cash. It always bothers me to have to do so. I'm always afraid I might somehow hurt the poor thing. Lord knows, I'd gag if someone stuck their fingers that far down my throat.

"Of course you know that the Congressman comes up for reelection next year, and that he's already none too popular in these parts."

"Frankly, I hadn't thought much about it. So?"

Sam shrugged. "So maybe nothing. Or, maybe tangling with the protesters is a calculated move on his part."

I wrenched the last buck from my wallet. "Why on earth would he want to do that?"

He shrugged again. "Who knows why the English do anything?"

I snapped my purse shut. "Don't give me that, Sam. You're a Methodist now, for Pete's sake."

Sam slapped the palm of his hand to his forehead. "Ooh, that hurt, Magdalena. You know that when I married Dorothy she refused to change churches. Anyway, mark my words, it's the Congressman, not the hippies, who came here to stir up big trouble."

"So marked," I said.

Sam and I are definitely not kissing cousins. He wouldn't even help me carry the groceries to my car, and he refuses to let the shopping carts leave his store. When we were kids, he was the one at family reunions who put frogs down my back, or pushed me in the mud when I was wearing my Sunday best.

Mama and Papa may have entertained hopes that Sam and I would someday marry, but I certainly never did. Still, it came as a shock to all of us when Sam married Dorothy Gillman, a Methodist from New York State. Of course it was just as well that he did. Anybody with poor-enough judgment to marry a woman who used mascara, wore slacks, and painted her toenails a bright red was definitely not worth pining over. At least that's what Mama told me.

I put Sam's rudeness and bad judgment out of my mind and drove reluctantly over to the police station to see Chief Myers's assistant. When accosted, my people have traditionally turned the other cheek. This can make for a lot of sore cheeks, and doesn't necessarily put an end to the violence. I suppose there is merit in that, but it is no longer one of my ways.

Still, I had never before had occasion to visit the police station, and had no idea what to expect. I certainly didn't expect to see Melvin Stoltzfus, *the* Melvin Stoltzfus, sitting behind Chief Myers's desk. Jeff was going to pay for not telling me the name of his assistant. I squelched a brief fantasy about Tammy wearing slippery shoes when she peered over the edge of the falls.

"Melvin?"

"Yes, ma'am. Acting Chief Melvin Stoltzfus."

"It's Magdalena. Magdalena Yoder."

Melvin rotated his head slowly to look up at me with the largest eyes I have ever seen on a man. Something about the way in which he deliberately did it reminded me of a praying mantis. Perhaps it had something to do with his being kicked in the head by that bull. I hadn't remembered Melvin Stoltzfus looking quite like that before.

"Magdalena! I remember you. Aren't you Susannah's older sister?"

"I plead the Fifth Amendment."

"What?"

"Never mind. Melvin, any word yet on what exactly did happen to Miss Brown?"

"Who?"

"Miss Brown," I repeated patiently. "You know, the woman who, uh, unfortunately passed away out at my place last night."

Melvin stared at me for an interminable length of time. I had the distinct feeling he was sizing me up, undoubtedly trying to decide if I was a juicy-enough morsel for him to pounce on and devour.

"Well, Melvin, did the coroner's report come in yet or not? Chief Myers said you would know."

One of Melvin's eyes seemed to rotate ever so slightly, and independently, in its socket. "In the first place, the coroner's report would be confidential at this point, if foul play was suspected. But in the second place, for your information, since we're just coming out of Thanksgiving weekend, you can expect things to be a little behind schedule."

"How much behind schedule are we talking?" If Miss Brown was a childless orphan, a delay would actually be welcome. But if she had doting parents or a dozen grieving children, any or all of whom might at that very moment be seeing a lawyer, I'd best hustle my bustle off to see Alvin.

"Can't say how much behind schedule," said Melvin. His tongue darted out and flicked lightly over his almost nonexistent lips for a few seconds. "Some things are confidential."

"I agree," I said recklessly.

Melvin's roaming eye stopped in mid-rotation. "What's that supposed to mean?"

Foolishly, I couldn't resist one-upping Melvin Stoltzfus. I told him about Miss Brown's bogus phone numbers.

"Of course, that doesn't mean anything," Melvin scoffed. "I often get wrong numbers."

"Go figure," I said sweetly. "Look, Melvin, one of the numbers being wrong I can understand. But both of them?"

"You sure that this Jumbo Jim's chicken place was the same number that was on her registration form?"

"As sure as you're a Stoltzfus."

"And how much did you say a bucket of extra crispy cost?"

"I didn't, Melvin."

"Was this Miss Brown all you wanted to talk to me about?"

"No. I also want to report an attempted murder out at my place."

"Apparently you haven't been listening, Magdalena. The

coroner's report still is not in. It may be negligence on your part that we're looking at, not murder. You should be talking to Alvin, not me."

Alvin, Melvin, shmelvin. I've raised chickens with higher I.Q.s. "I'm not talking about Miss Brown anymore," I said, with perhaps a slight note of exasperation in my voice. "What I mean is, today somebody tried to kill me."

"I see." He pulled some forms out of a drawer, picked up a ballpoint, and sat poised like he was getting ready to take a timed exam.

"Don't you want to hear the details?"

He smiled placidly. The skin on the left side of his face was pulled tight and there appeared to be an indentation just inside his hairline. Perhaps that's where he had been kicked in the head. "Before we get into the details, I need some background information on you."

"What information? Melvin, you've known me all my life."

"Name?"

"You already know that!"

Melvin was as persistent as a sweat fly in August.

"Name?"

"Oh, all right. Magdalena Yoder."

"Middle name?"

"Won't an initial do?" It's bad enough that my mother named me after a packet of flower seeds. She could at least have nixed the Latin.

"Middle name?"

"Portulaca. But breathe that to a single soul and—"

"Age?"

"Thirty-nine."

"Age?"

"Forty-three. But what does this have to do with my being shot at?"

"Sex?"

"Never! I mean it's none of your business."

"Sex?"

After Melvin had garnered all my personal statistics, except for my bra and shoe size (which are not the same, no matter what Freni says), he finally let me tell him about the incident.

"You don't allow hunting on your land, do you?" he interrupted me at one point.

"Of course not."

"Then that couldn't have been a hunter on your land."

"How's that?"

Melvin was on a roll. "And you don't know why anyone would want to kill you, do you?"

"To spare me these questions?"

He began to rub his hands together rhythmically. "If you don't know why someone would want to kill you, then there probably wasn't anyone trying to kill you. And we know it wasn't a hunter. So, either you are mistaken about being shot at or you are lying to me, Magdalena, and just wasting my time." He rolled his huge eyes into position and gazed up at me like a monstrous mantis. "And I know you don't lie, Magdalena Yoder. Do you?"

"You forgot Portulaca."

"Do you?"

There was no stopping such persistence. I decided to get

out of there before he devoured me. "I don't suppose you know the name of the hotel Chief Myers is staying at in Niagara Falls, do you?"

Melvin turned his head slowly to an impossible angle. Quite possibly he was trying to point with his chin. "The sign on this desk says 'Melvin Stoltzfus.' That's me. I'm in charge while the Chief's away. Got any more questions?"

"No, so in that case I guess I'll just be going. Thanks for everything."

The bulging blue-gray eyes seemed to have focused on me before his head had fully turned back into position. "It's quite all right, Magdalena, but next time try not to let your imagination get the best of you."

"Bull!" I said. That said it all.

# Chapter Fourteen

Susannah and Shnookums were in the kitchen when I returned. I didn't actually see Shnookums, but since he is never a dog's breath away from her, I knew he was there. Susannah, at least, appeared to be making toast and coffee.

"What's the matter? Can't sleep anymore?" I asked pleasantly enough.

Susannah rolled her eyes, which for her is a fairly tolerant gesture. "I am not the lazy thing you think I am, Mags. I've been up for at least forty-five minutes, doing my nails."

A quick glance at the wall clock told me it was seven minutes till one. Just as I'd thought. Only sinners are capable of sleeping past noon.

"And besides which," she continued, "I'm working right now. I'm making lunch for Her Highness."

"What? Is Jeanette back already?"

"Not that Her Highness. Mrs. Ream."

"Lydia came back already?"

Susannah opened the fridge and got out some cottage cheese and hard-boiled eggs. "She never left in the first place. Scared me to death when I saw her. I was coming downstairs for a Pepsi and Little Debbies when I ran into her on the stairs. We both nearly fell down those damned stairs and broke our necks we were so frightened."

"Susannah!"

"Well, do you want to hear the juicy details, or what?"

I sold out my principles for the juicy details. "Do tell."

Susannah talked while she fixed Lydia's plate. "I asked Mrs. Ream why she was back already and she told me she'd never left. Said she hadn't been feeling so well after breakfast, a stomach thing, and thought she should stick close to the house. She also said she'd started to feel a little better and had gone out for a short walk. Just to look at the barn and stuff. Only I don't think that's the whole truth."

"What do you mean?" I have to hand it to Susannah. She attracts interesting bits of news like black wool attracts lint.

"Well, for one thing, there's that fight she had with her husband this morning. I think it's Garrett, not diarrhea, that kept her home. Although, how can you tell the difference?"

"Susannah!"

"Well, you know what I mean." She poured coffee from the percolator into a small serving pot. "Anyway, after I re-covered from shock on the stairs, I noticed there were some pine needles caught in her hair." Susannah paused and waited for me to say something.

Eventually I obliged. "So?"

"So! Mags, the only pine trees we've got on the farm are back in the woods. It's all maples up by the house, and there aren't any trees by the barn. So don't you think the woods is a wee bit far to go if you've got the runs?"

"You've got a point," I said excitedly. "And if Lydia was in the woods, she might have seen someone, or at least could verify that shots had been fired."

Susannah put a little pot of homemade boysenberry jam and a salt and pepper set on the tray. "Except that she came back from her walk several hours after you claimed you were shot at."

"Not claimed—was!"

"All right, was. My point is that she couldn't have heard the shots or seen anyone, because she wasn't even in the woods then."

"Yeah, I guess you're right. Say, you're not the only one with news. Guess who I saw in town?"

"Your old boyfriend, Sam?" Susannah pointed to the bags of produce that I still had not bothered to put away. After all, there was no hurry. How limp can Sam's bok choy get?

"That's not who I mean. I saw"—I paused for dramatic effect—"Melvin Stoltzfus!"

"Our new acting Police Chief."

"You knew?"

"It was in the paper, Mags. You really ought to get more in touch with the world."

"That's not fair! I read."

"Yeah, books. But not important stuff. Isn't Melvin cute?"

"Cute? You think Melvin Stoltzfus is cute?"

"You're always too hard on people, Magdalena. You're far too picky. Even Mama used to say so. Melvin's got the most adorable eyes. You know—bedroom eyes they call them."

"I wouldn't think there'd be room for his eyes in my bed," I said, perhaps cruelly.

"There you go! Running people down. That's why there's never been anybody in your bed, Magdalena. And probably never will be."

"That's not true at all. I don't sleep with men because I'm not married. It's as simple as that. And even if I were to throw my morals to the wind and be a slut, like some people I know, I wouldn't go to bed with someone who has to use his fingers to count to ten."

Susannah slammed some silverware down on the tray. "Melvin never got kicked by any damned cow. That story was just made up by Sarah Berkey because he jilted her."

"Bull."

"What?"

"Never mind, just take the tray up to Lydia." It's a hard lesson for me to learn, but if I bite my tongue hard enough, and think of Mama turning over in her grave, I can sometimes extricate myself from our arguments before it's too late.

"I'm gone!" shouted Susannah. Then, too studied to be an afterthought, she turned with the tray and gave me what I suppose she thought was a coy wink. "I almost forgot to tell you, Mags, but you had a phone call."

"I did not switch the prices on Sam's salad dressings," I said, perhaps a bit too defensively.

"Not Sam. This was from a man, a Jim something. Big Jim, I think it was. Anyway, he wouldn't leave a message, except that he'd call back sometime. And he called you doll!"

Susannah laughed like a blithering idiot and ran upstairs with the tray containing hot coffee. How is it that she managed to negotiate those impossibly steep stairs at high speed and not even spill a drop of java, whereas poor little Miss Brown ended up like a sack of potatoes at their foot? A sack of *mashed* potatoes.

I decided not to dwell on that morbid subject any longer, nor did I particularly want to think about Jumbo Jim's call. My brief conversation with him had been far too much fun. If it involves a man, and is fun, it has got to be wrong, or so Mama always told me. When your mind starts to get too busy, or filled with unwelcome thoughts, the only way to clear it is to roll up your sleeves and get your hands dirty. Dirty hands, you can always wash. A dirty mind, however, is a first-class ticket to hell.

I left the groceries where they were and went out back to help Mose shovel out the henhouse. We do it twice a year, when the weather's not too cold, but cold enough so that it moderates the fumes from the acrid droppings. The fall rakings, which include a lot of straw, are spread over the vegetable patch, and come spring, it's tame enough to make a lovely fertilizer. The spring rakings go on the compost heap. By late summer they've mellowed enough to assist the fall crop.

Our chickens are range fed, which means they don't spend a lot of time in the henhouse, except at night, or to lay. Often there's no one at home when we shovel. There's something therapeutic, almost religious, about shoveling excrement in an empty henhouse twice a year. It's not only humbling, but in addition to cleaning the joint, I usually feel like my soul has been somehow cleansed as well. Of course, it may be just the fumes.

"Say, Mose," I began, once the job was done, "did you see Mrs. Ream, the Congressman's wife, taking a walk this morning?"

Mose shook his head. "I didn't see any of the English this morning."

"Well, that's strange, because Mrs. Ream told Susannah she went out for a walk by the barn after breakfast."

Mose took off his straw hat and wiped his forehead with his coat sleeve. "I didn't see any of the English," he repeated, "but there was someone out by the barn."

"You heard someone?"

"No. Matilda did." Matilda Holsteincoo is one of our two remaining cows. To hear Mose talk, you'd think they were the daughters he never had.

"What do you mean Matilda did?"

"She wouldn't let down her milk for the longest time. It makes her nervous, you know, if someone else is there."

"What about Bertha? Was she nervous too?"

Mose knew I was teasing him, but as usual he never let on. "Bertha knows no shame. She gave even more than usual."

"That hussy!"

Mose smiled despite himself. Then his face darkened. "Magdalena, which one of the English does that car belong to?" He pointed to the asphalt-gray jalopy once owned by the deceased Miss Brown.

"Ah, that belonged to the woman who accidentally fell down our stairs. Heather Brown. Why do you ask?"

"I don't know much about cars, Magdalena, but that one's broken in back. Where you put stuff. I think it happened here."

"You mean the trunk?"

"That's what I mean."

We walked over to the car to take a closer look. Sure enough, the trunk lid was open. The evidence suggested that it had been forced. There were scratch marks around the keyhole, and along the bottom of the trunk lid there was a series of indentations. It would have been obvious even to Melvin's mother that someone had used a crowbar to force it open.

"What makes you think it happened here?"

"It didn't look like that yesterday."

"You sure?"

I thought I saw Mose blush. "I'm sure. I had my eye on that one. If Freni and I were ever to get a car, it would be one like that, I think. Not too worldly. Of course, we would paint it black."

"Of course."

I peered into the trunk. It was empty. If there had been something worth the trouble to force it open, it was no longer there. The floor of the trunk was carpeted, gray of course, and, as I would have expected from Miss Brown, must have been recently vacuumed. But then, just as I was turning away, something caught my eye. Just inside the trunk, almost hidden by the curve of metal that formed the rear lip, was a single sunflower seed. Once I saw it, it was as obvious as a diamond on a coal heap.

Mose saw it too. "The Englishman. The tall, skinny Englishman. He eats seeds like that."

For some reason I felt immediately defensive of young Joel Teitlebaum. "One swallow does not a summer make," I countered. "And besides, Mose, does he seem like the type who could jimmy this open with a crowbar?"

"Freni could."

I politely rolled my eyes by turning my head away first. "Freni could do anything, Mose. She was born on a farm. I doubt if Joel could even open one of Freni's jars of pickled watermelon rinds. I think it was someone else, trying to make it look like Joel. It seems too obvious to me."

"What do you mean?"

I told Mose about the fire escape door being left open, and the trail of sunflower seed shells.

Mose pointed to the gravel at our feet. "Well, whoever it was, they chewed tobacco too."

Then I noticed the glob of still-damp spittle containing tobacco fragments. Hernia is filled with tobacco chewers, not to mention consummate spitters of all kinds.

"It was an outsider," I said. It had to be. I couldn't imagine the Congressman, or Delbert, chawing down on a wad. And Joel was far too much of a health freak to do such a thing. Billy Dee came the closest to fitting the profile of a chaw chomper, but he was too much of a gentleman to break into anyone's car trunk. Especially a woman's.

"Maybe you should call the Chief," suggested Mose.

I shook my head and practically stamped my feet. "The Chief's off in Canada catching fish and saving his wife from going over Niagara Falls. Melvin Stoltzfus is his replacement."

"*The* Melvin Stoltzfus?" asked Mose incredulously.

"I'm afraid so."

"I heard that old bull he tried to milk will never be the same. He moos in falsetto now."

Old Mose didn't even have a twinkle in his eye, so clearly he believed the story. Of course I didn't. "Mose, I think we should just try and wire the trunk lid shut the best we can and say nothing. Who knows why an outsider would want to break into Miss Brown's trunk, but Melvin sure isn't going to know either. So why borrow trouble, right?"

"Melvin is trouble. I'll see if I can tie down the trunk. But, Magdalena, I need to ask you a question."

"Ask away, Mose."

"Can Freni have her job back? You know how she is when she's not working."

"Can it be any worse than when she is working?" I tried to laugh pleasantly. "Okay, I suppose so, Mose."

His face lit up. "You aren't too mad at Freni, Magdalena?"

"Of course I'm mad, but I'll get over it. I always do."

"Good. You are like the daughter she never had. She is very fond of you, Magdalena. She doesn't really mean what she says. She just has trouble with her temper."

"Like me?"

He flushed. "I didn't say that."

I looked over at the field where Matilda and Bertha were peacefully grazing. "Tell her she's welcome back anytime. All she has to do is apologize."

Mose shook his head ruefully and headed silently for the barn. We both knew it would be a sweet-smelling day in the henhouse before Freni Hostetler said "sorry" to me.


I had just put away the last of the groceries when the first of the guests returned. The first one I saw, anyway, was Billy Dee, who came bounding into the kitchen in search of something cold to drink. Having been in the woods definitely seemed to agree with him.

"I take it their protest was not successful then?" I asked, as I handed him a glass of Bertha's milk. Or was it the shy Matilda's?

"Heck no, Miss Yoder. We didn't see hide nor hair of them folks the whole day."

"Which, of course, was none of your doing."

"Exactly. It weren't my fault we got lost twice on our way to the game lands, even if I was leading the way, and it certainly weren't my fault we parked on the opposite side of the ridge from the Congressman. And when we did go into the woods for just a bit, someone took a potshot at Jeanette." He laughed heartily. "That really weren't my fault."

"Someone shot at Jeanette?"

He was still laughing. "Maybe it was a bear hunter! She sure don't look like a deer to me!"

"Mr. Grizzle! You of all people!"

Billy Dee sobered immediately. "You're right. I should be the last one to find this funny. I guess it's just my nerves working themselves off. Coming up here ain't no picnic for me. It's just something I had to do."

"Was Jeanette hurt?" It wouldn't be so bad if she got hurt just a little bit, would it? Nothing serious, mind you, but just enough to send her packing.

"Hurt? Nah, she was gabbing so loud she didn't even know she was shot at. Not till I pointed it out. Bullet came whistling right past her head and hit an old stump nearby. I dug it out." He reached into his pocket and produced a shiny lump of metal. "Funny thing is, this ain't no rifle bullet. This is from a revolver. A Smith & Wesson .44 Magnum, if you ask me."

"You mean to say that someone tried to kill her? That it wasn't a stray hunter's bullet?"

He nodded. "Course, I didn't tell her that. I just said there was some blind fool of a hunter in the vicinity and the wisest thing was for us to get back to the car."

"And?"

He sighed. "And she agreed, after she'd made a few comments that I'd just as soon not remember. That woman has all the sensitivity of a brood sow in heat. Oops. No offense, Miss Yoder."

"No offense taken. Drink your milk," I ordered. "It's the best thing there is for nerves. Say, you wouldn't happen to cook, would you?"

He smiled gratefully. "I make a mean venison stew. Why?"

I crossed my fingers under the kitchen table. "Well, tonight's Monday night, of course, and that's our traditional night for potluck suppers. You see, everyone at the table has to make their own favorite dish to share. Of course, you wouldn't be making venison stew because we don't have any, but—"

"But I do."

"What?"

He smiled broadly, like the old Billy Dee Grizzle. The milk must have taken its effect. "That ain't no problem at all. Got me an eight-pointer tied to the roof of my car right now."

"You what? I thought you gave up hunting."

"Well, now, I didn't shoot it. I picked this one up alongside the road. With all that shooting going on, them deer crowd the road for safety, and every now and then one of them gets just a little too close. Like this one done."

I nearly gagged. "You mean you want to make road-kill stew right here in my kitchen?"

Billy Dee looked almost hurt. "This here ain't no run-of-the-mill road-kill, Miss Yoder. There's hardly a scratch on it, and besides, it was as warm and red as a fresh-baked cherry pie when I picked it up."

"Thank you. Cherry pie will never be the same again."

"What?"

"Nothing. Did anybody else see you pick up the deer?"

"Not a soul. I was the last car to leave, and by the time I pulled up here, they'd all gone in."

Call me daring or just plain foolish, but I'd already survived two whizzing bullets and was feeling surprisingly adventuresome. "Quickly, pull your car around the back side of the barn. I'll go open the main door. You skin and gut it in there."

The look on Billy Dee's face was priceless. "Don't that take all!"

"Of course, you'll do a good job of cleaning up in there when you're done, and you won't breathe a word of this to anyone?"

"I swear! I mean, yes, ma'am!"

By the time I'd squared Billy Dee away in the barn, and watched him at work for a while, the Congressman and his aide had returned. One by one, I cornered the guests and gave them my spiel about it being potluck night, and, much to my great surprise, one by one they volunteered dishes. Even Jeanette was cheerful and cooperative, which only goes to show you that a near miss by a bullet can do wonders for one's morale.

The Congressman volunteered to make Senate Bean Soup, but since he didn't have time to soak the beans, he settled on a doctored-up version of canned baked beans.

Lydia said she knew a wonderful recipe for vegetable curry she was sure everyone would like.

"But I don't have curry powder," I explained. "The Amish aren't big on exotic Oriental dishes."

"Well, do you have cinnamon, nutmeg, ginger, coriander, cumin, garlic, and chili?"

"Everything but cumin."

"Then I can make my own curry. A cumin-less curry unfortunately, but still a curry."

Happily, I found the spices for her. You have to admire a woman who knows how to make her own curry powder, that's for sure.

Joel, bless his heart, was as flexible as a willow twig in April. Before I'd even told him about the produce haul, he was all set to make something.

"You do have potatoes?" It was more of a statement than a question.

"Of course!"

"Apple sauce?"

"Organic to the core."

"And sour cream, for those who want it?"

"That would be Matilda's. She's the nervous one."

"I beg your pardon?"

"Never mind. What are you making?"

"Latkes. Jewish potato pancakes. After all, in just six more weeks it will be Chanukah."

"Bless you."

"That will be my main dish contribution. Then for dessert, I'd like to make my famous broiled bananas."

"Double bless you."

Linda wasn't quite as cooperative as I'd expected, at least not until I'd mentioned that Sam had sold me some six different varieties of leafy green things with foreign-sounding names.

"There's a Belgian something, a Swiss something, a Roman something—or was that Romanian?"

"Well, I might put together a nice fresh salad," she conceded.

I decided not to clarify the fresh part. "Great! And I have lots of dressing in the fridge."

Linda looked like I must have when Billy Dee mentioned his road-kill. "You mean commercial, bottled dressings?"

"Yeah. Brand names even."

"Hmm. I do have an hour of hatha-yoga this afternoon, and Ms. Parker did want me to do some channeling before dinner. Perhaps I have just enough time to make up a bottle of natural dressing. Without preservatives in it. You wouldn't happen to have organic dandelion vinegar and fresh tarragon, would you?"

"I think there's some dandelion vinegar in the cellar," I said. "On a shelf, way in the back corner. There's a flashlight by the cellar door you can use."

Sometimes when I'm nasty like that, I wonder if I'm adopted. Neither Mama nor Papa would have, for even a second, considered sending an arachnophobiac down into a cellar swarming with spiders. But so help me, some people deserve what they get.

Jeanette had already volunteered to make a vegetarian stir-fried dish, providing, of course, I could come up with some fresh, crisp vegetables. With my fingers crossed, I assured her I had.

That left only Delbert, Susannah, and me. I, however, didn't plan to make anything, because I would have more than my hands full supervising everybody else in my kitchen. Besides which, I'd already cooked breakfast, packed lunches, washed dishes, been shot at, shopped, matched wits with a witless lawman, shoveled offal, and watched Billy Dee butcher a battered buck. There's only so much a body can do in one day. Fortunately, Joel had volunteered to make two dishes, so mine wouldn't even be missed.

Delbert James, as it turned out, was just as generous. He graciously offered to cook two dishes as well, but I reluctantly turned him down. While I knew I would love his macaroni and ground-beef casserole, I wasn't too sure I could handle the tripe and suet pudding he proposed, even though he offered to go into town himself to pick up the ingredients. Delbert James, I was forced to conclude, had humbler origins than one might normally expect of a Congressman's aide.

As for Susannah, her concept of nutrition is taken straight from the Freni Hostetler School of Cooking. If it tastes good, eat it. Unfortunately, her boiled cookies were the only thing nobody got to sample that night.

# Chapter Fifteen

### SUSANNAH YODER ENTWHISTLE'S
### BOILED COOKIE RECIPE

2 cups sugar
3 tablespoons cocoa powder
⅓ cup milk
½ cup chunky peanut butter
1 teaspoon vanilla
1 stick margarine
3 cups rolled quick oats

Mix the sugar, cocoa, and milk together in a heavy pot. Boil
for one minute.

Stir in the peanut butter, vanilla, and margarine.

Remove from heat and add the rolled oats, mixing well.

Using a teaspoon, drop the still-warm mixture by the
spoonful onto waxed paper.

When cool, peel off the waxed paper and enjoy.

# Chapter Sixteen

It got a little crowded in the kitchen around six p.m. Since Billy Dee Grizzle had a stew to make, he'd got there first and had appropriated the left front burner of our six-burner, institutional stove. Billy had started browning his meat around five, and by six his stew was well underway, filling the kitchen with a heady, but not altogether disagreeable odor.

Delbert James was the next cook on the scene. His macaroni-hamburger casserole required some stove-top cooking in its initial stages, but was eventually transferred to the oven to bake. The cheese-topped concoction was already merrily bubbling and browning away in the oven when Jeanette and Lydia showed up at the same time.

"What the hell is that stench?" demanded Jeanette. "This room is fouled with the odor of simmering flesh."

"It smells delicious to me," said Lydia firmly.

"Just how the hell am I supposed to cook with that stuff stinking up the joint?"

"No need to," said Billy Dee warmly, "there's plenty in this pot to go around. Just put up your dogs and relax for a spell. Let us men do the cooking."

"Like hell I will."

Normally I didn't tell my guests how to talk, but this was Mama's kitchen, and poor Mama had already done enough turning over for the day. If someone didn't make Jeanette put a lid on it, Mama would soon be spinning so fast she might start generating electricity.

"I don't allow swearing on these premises, Ms. Parker," I said as graciously as I could.

Jeanette's face turned as red as her hair, but she shut up for a minute. I wish Lydia had.

"What's in your pot, Mr. Grizzle?" she asked politely.

Billy lifted the lid and deeply inhaled the escaping steam. "Venison stew, ma'am."

"Deer meat?"

"That, and a few onions, carrots, and spuds."

"Bambi?" Jeanette almost shrieked. "You're cooking Bambi?"

"I knew a Bambi once," said Billy Dee pleasantly. "Things were definitely cooking with her."

"That's disgusting, and so is your stew. I thought you'd given up hunting, Mr. Grizzle. After what you did to your daughter."

A muscle in Billy's left cheek twitched slightly, but other than that, he managed to keep his cool. "I have given up hunting, Ms. Parker. This is just something I scraped up off the road."

Jeanette looked as if she were about ready to toss her cookies. Instead, she tossed her flaming red hair out of her eyes, stomped over to the fridge, and demanded to see what vegetables I'd come up with. Humbly I showed her.

"You call that bok choy? That's as limp as Delbert James's wrist."

"Hey, I heard that," Delbert called from his position by the stove. Surprisingly, he didn't seem at all miffed. If anything, he sounded amused. I, for one, was not amused. It meant that Susannah had got her information right, and that Billy Dee probably did have a girlfriend. Not that it concerned me, of course.

"And are those supposed to be Chinese pea pods? I've seen pureed vegetables crisper than these!" shouted Jeanette.

"Children, children," said Lydia gently. She turned to me. "Would you happen to have any clarified butter, Miss Yoder? I need it for the curry."

I confessed that all my butter was blurry. "Can you make your curry without butter? Then maybe everyone will eat it."

Lydia smiled patiently. "But the curry contains yogurt. If they won't eat butter, they certainly won't eat yogurt."

"Keeping animals penned up is a form of slavery, and forcibly taking milk from them is a form of abuse," Jeanette butted in, "possibly even sexual abuse. And besides which, dairy products clog one's arteries, not to mention, milk is a leading cause of flatulence."

"Do you have any olive oil then?" asked Lydia graciously. How I admired that woman!

"Yes, I do," I said happily. I normally don't stock the stuff, but this bottle was left behind by a guest, an Italian count, who had a fetish for anything extra virgin. The two-liter bottle he left behind was hardly compensation for all the times he chased me around the Inn. Had he not been an octogenarian, or at least a little cuter, he might have caught me.

"Good. Olive oil will do just fine," the saintly woman said.

That settled, we all set back to work. In a few minutes we were joined by Joel and Garrett. Then by a disgruntled Linda.

"There isn't any dandelion vinegar in the cellar, Ms. Yoder. Just millions and millions of horrible spiders. You must call an exterminator!"

I could see that she was shaken, and her face was the color of a peeled leek bulb, but I hadn't heard any screams. "Are you sure you went all the way to the back, to those shelves behind the furnace?"

"Ms. Yoder, even Indiana Jones couldn't do that! The place is crawling with those things. I insist that you call an exterminator."

Those were pretty strong words coming from a mere snippet of a kid, if you ask me. "Ms. McMahon, I am shocked at how you talk. And I thought you reverenced life! Killing spiders, indeed. What, pray tell, is worse? To kill a nasty old cow for food, or to slaughter an entire community of innocent insects?"

"Spiders are not insects! And they aren't innocent. They're horrible!"

"Have you ever been bitten by one?"

"No."

"Mugged, raped, or otherwise accosted?"

"Very funny," said Jeanette. That woman butts into more things than a drunken billy goat. "Leave the poor kid alone. She's absolutely right. This place is a dump. What a dump!"

"Bette Davis you're not," said Delbert gaily.

"But dumpy's another thing." I think I said that.

"What?"

"If you don't have any basmati rice, then ordinary long grain will do," said the ever vigilant and cooperative Lydia.

"Now where are those canned beans I'm supposed to doctor up?" asked Garrett impatiently.

Before I could reply, Susannah and Shnookums meandered in. At first I could only assume that Shnookums had accompanied her, but it would have been a safe bet. Susannah was wearing enough yardage to conceal a Great Dane. Just thinking that made me count my blessings. If Shnookums had been a Great Dane, those wouldn't have been pellets I found on my pillow the week before.

Billy obligingly transferred his stew to a cast-iron Dutch oven, which he then stuck in the oven, so as to open up more stove-top space. I made Susannah say thank you.

Because Susannah is anything but competent, and claims to be more anemic than a perpetual blood donor, I myself got out the huge pot for her cookies. Susannah did, after all, want to make a double batch.

Susannah's recipe only requires a few minutes at the stove, but my sister was determined to make them count. Quite unexpectedly, she burst into a high-pitched wail. I'm sure the sound startled everyone in the room but me, who immediately recognized it as a tune from the centuries-old hymnal, the *Ausbund*. This isn't even a Mennonite hymn, but an Amish one, and I can only guess that Susannah's motive was to give her captive audience the authentic flavor of Pennsylvania Dutch life, which her cooking couldn't deliver.

That Susannah even remembered the hymn surprised me. Mama used to sing it to me as a child, but I am ten years older than Susannah, and I can't remember Mama singing it after I reached my teens. At any rate, the hymn, like many others in the *Ausbund,* sounds more like keening than singing to English ears. And while Susannah's rendition was neither musically nor lyrically accurate, it definitely was loud.

I scurried over to the stove to tell her to put a lid on it, before someone else did. But before I could even open my mouth, Susannah opened hers even wider. What seconds before had been keening was now genuine screaming. I'm sure that at first I was the only one who could tell the difference.

I grabbed her by the shoulders and turned her around. "What is it?"

Susannah wrenched free and faced the pot again, her screams louder than ever. Then she began to gesticulate wildly at the pot, almost as if she were trying to do the breaststroke. Perhaps there was something about the pot that was not quite right. I bent over and examined its contents closely. Then it was all I could do to keep from screaming myself.

There, blinking up at me, totally covered with chocolate and peanut butter, was Shnookums. His little mouth was open too, and he would have been screaming as well, except that it was clogged with peanut butter.

Without even thinking, I yanked the pot off the burner and dumped its contents into the sink. Then I turned on the cold-water faucet as far as it would go and aimed the sprayer hose at the half-cooked canine. Susannah, in the meantime, had fainted. Fortunately, Billy Dee managed to grab her before she had a chance to slump over the stove.

"What the hell is going on now?" Jeanette demanded.

"Go away!" I snapped. The cold water wasn't doing much

to dissolve the hot goo from the dog's coat. I switched to warm.

Jeanette pushed into my space. "What the hell is that? I demand to know. My God, it's a rat!" she shrieked. She too began to faint, but when nobody made a move to catch her, she revived in time to brace herself against the sink.

"This is not a rat!" I shouted, so that everyone could hear. "This is Shnookums, my sister's dog."

Linda gasped, and although my back was turned, I'm sure she tried her hand at fainting too. "First spiders," I heard her say, "and now rats. I'm calling the board of health myself."

Just about then, I stuck my finger in the little dog's mouth and dislodged a glob of peanut butter. Immediately I heard Shnookums wheeze, and then his little chest began to move up and down. Seconds later he was revived enough to let loose with the most pitiful yowl I have ever heard. Even I felt sorry for the matted mutt.

"It is a dog!" I heard Lydia say.

"Rats can sound like that too," Jeanette and Linda said together.

Susannah had, by then, regained consciousness and was struggling to her feet. Billy Dee, ever the gentleman, was concerned that she might collapse again and was trying to coax her to remain prone. "Please lie still, Miss Entwhistle," he begged. "You're paler than a Yankee come February."

"Let me go!" she screamed. "That's my baby over there!"

At the sound of his mistress's voice, Shnookums began to wail even louder.

Reluctantly Billy Dee helped Susannah to her feet and walked her over to the sink. By then I had managed to do a fair job of cleaning the canine, and he bore at least a faint resemblance to Shnookums. Of course, any small animal, dog or cat, looks half their size when wet. Frankly, I've seen rats twice the size of the soggy Shnookums.

"See! It is a rat!" shrieked Jeanette. "It fell right from the ceiling into that pot. God knows what all we'll be eating tonight."

"I think I'm going to be sick," moaned Linda.

Susannah grabbed her baby out of my hands and held him to her face for close inspection. He continued to wail. She began planting kisses all over his tiny body. He wailed even louder.

"I think you'd best take him to the vet," suggested Billy Dee.

Now Susannah began to wail. "My baby, my poor little baby, and it's all your fault!"

I think she meant me. After all, it had been my idea that she cook something for supper. Of course she wasn't being fair, but this was no time to point it out.

"I'll get our coats and then we're heading straight for Doc Shafer," I said calmly. "Lydia, would you mind seeing to it that supper gets on the table and everyone gets a chance to eat? Mr. Grizzle, would you please call Dr. Shafer and tell him we're coming? I think he closes at six. His number is by the phone at the front desk."

Papa would have been proud of me for my level-headedness. I think I got that quality from him. Anyway, acting calm in a crisis and delegating responsibility seem to come naturally to me, except when something really serious comes along, like being shot at. Papa always used to say I should become a manager and manage something, like a business or an organization. Susannah, on the other hand, says I should manage my own business. Mama probably agreed more with Susannah than with Papa, but she was too gentle ever to say such a thing.

While Susannah and Shnookums wailed, I calmly drove them to Doc Shafer's, who lives six miles on the other side of Hernia. Old Doc is primarily a farm vet, whose specialty is delivering breech births in cows. Doc has been treating our livestock since before I was born. In recent years, however, his arthritis has prevented his getting down on his knees and reaching up the birth canal of a Holstein, so he's shifted his focus to treating pets.

"Evening, ladies," said Doc cheerfully.

Neither Susannah nor Shnookums were at all coherent, so I filled Doc in on all the details. "I immediately got the chocolate mixture off and rinsed him with cool water," I concluded.

"You did fine, Magdalena. I always said you would have made a good veterinarian."

I felt myself blushing. By and large I get fewer compliments than Saddam Hussein. "Thanks, Doc. Are the burns bad?"

He shook his head. "As far as I can tell, mostly first degree. With these smaller breeds, the problem is shock as much as anything else. What I'd like to do is give him a sedative and keep him overnight for observation. But I think he'll be as good as new by tomorrow."

You would have thought I'd plopped her pooch in a bun and smeared him with mustard the way Susannah carried on. "I won't leave without my baby!" she screamed. "My baby! My precious little itsy-bitsy baby! My Shnookums Wookums!" I

had never, ever seen an adult woman carry on that way. If she
had been a character in a movie or a book, someone would
have slapped her silly to get her to stop. Although I doubt if it
would have done any good.

"What you really need to do is give Susannah a sedative,"
I couldn't help saying.

"I could give her a shot of something to calm her down,"
Doc agreed. He gestured at the rows of bottles on the shelves
behind him.

"Would that be legal?" I asked hopefully. "I mean, I don't
want to be doing anything wrong."

Old Doc smiled. "I'll be eighty-two next month. If they
take my license away, I'll retire. So, who are you going to trust,
me or the legislators?"

I thought for a second about Garrett Ream, and decided to
choose Doc. It was either that or leave Susannah with him for
the night. I simply did not have the energy to sit up with her
screaming all night.

"Stick it to her," I said.

Susannah never saw it coming, but undoubtedly she felt it.
But only for a second. Almost immediately her screams faded
to sobs, and then weak little whimpers. Amazingly,
Shnookums quieted down too, and soon it would have been
impossible to tell, had I been wearing a blindfold, which sound
was coming from whom.

"Are you sure she'll be all right?"

"She'll sleep like a baby. Actually, maybe more like a
lamb. That was my best sheep tranquilizer."

"Thanks, Doc."

"Say," he began almost shyly, "I've got some baked ham

and scalloped potatoes in the back. I don't suppose you'd join me for supper?"

Doc's wife, the former Anna Speicher, had been dead for seventeen years. In the old days, Mama used to invite Doc to stay for supper all the time. Daddy used to tease Mama and say it was because Doc was easy on the eyes, but I'm sure it was more than that. Mama had a soft spot for anyone who was lonely or needy, and besides which, Anna Speicher Shafer and Mama were third cousins. Even without any "removeds."

So when old Doc returned the favor, it didn't take me long to accept. Especially not after I let a quick vision of the bunch back at the PennDutch flit across my brain. "What about Susannah?" I asked.

"She'll be just fine on the sofa in there. That way we can keep an eye on her vital signs for a while before you take her home."

He put the now quiet Shnookums in a cage and I helped him get Susannah to the couch. Then Doc and I settled down and had a good old-fashioned meal, like the kind we were meant to eat. In addition to the ham and scalloped potatoes, Doc served up green beans with bacon, dried corn pudding, and rhubarb-strawberry pie. Both the rhubarb and the beans, he confessed, had been canned last spring.

"Do you eat like this all the time?" I asked in amazement.

Doc waited until he had swallowed a bite of freshly baked roll dripping with butter before he answered. "Guess I have to. I live to eat, and if the eating's not worthwhile, I may as well just give up and die."

"Some people say they just eat to live," I countered.

Old Doc snorted. "Then they're sick."

"Pardon me?"

"It's a fact, at least with animals. If something doesn't like to eat, chances are it's sick."

"Pass the ham, please," I said quickly, proving I was healthy as a horse.

Doc smiled approvingly. "Makes my heart glad to see a woman eat like that, Magdalena. It's a sure sign of passion, you know."

Somehow I doubted it. "Look, Doc, I have to ask you something."

"Then ask away." The old geezer was waving a spoon full of scalloped potatoes seductively in front of me. Of course, then it all made sense. Old Doc must have been sweet on Mama too, and Mama had made Roseanne Barr look like a barrette.

I ignored the proffered spuds. "It's this, Doc. I suppose you've already heard about the woman who took a tumble out at the Inn."

He nodded.

"Well, Chief Myers says it might have been an accident, and it might have been foul play. But if it was an accident, Doc, I could be sued for everything I've got. I might even lose the Inn!"

"Says who?"

"Well, Melvin Stoltzfus, for one."

Doc snorted. "That boy couldn't find his way south from the North Pole. It seems to me, Magdalena, that you'd really have a problem if the other scenario was true."

"You mean that nobody would want to stay at a place where someone had been killed?"

"That might come later. But for now, I'd say your biggest

worry should be that you just might have a killer staying at the Inn."

"You mean *now?*"

Doc's look was all the answer I needed. Melvin, move over. Why hadn't I seen the ramifications myself? "Why didn't Chief Myers make that a bit clearer to me?" I asked, as soon as I could speak.

"What? And spoil a perfectly good fishing trip?" asked Doc. He didn't sound like he was kidding.

I temporarily hoped that Tammy Myers not only stood too near Niagara Falls, but that she managed to pull the Chief in with her when she fell. I filled Doc in on a number of things.

Doc listened intently, but he seemed to be most interested in Jumbo Jim's Fried Chicken and Seafood Palace. "How much *is* a bucket of extra crispy?" he asked, interrupting my narrative.

"Too much to go driving two hundred and fifty miles for," I snapped.

"Easy, girl, easy," said Doc. "I sense I've hit a nerve. How long did you talk to this guy?"

"I'll let you know when I get my phone bill."

"That long, huh?" Doc sounded like he just might be jealous.

"And he called me once, but I was out," I said just to be nasty.

"How did he get your number?" Doc was definitely jealous.

"Beats me. Susannah took the message. Say, Doc, do you want to hear the rest of what's been going on, or not?"

"Sure," said Doc. "Anyway, Baltimore is a long ways away. You won't be hearing from this guy again."

I ignored Doc's last comment and proceeded to tell him

how I had found the fire escape door open, and that the trunk of Miss Brown's car had been broken into. Of course, I pointed out, it was possible, even probable, that neither of those things had anything to do with Miss Brown's becoming intimate with my impossibly steep stairs.

"Nonetheless, do you want me coming back to stay the night?" Doc asked kindly.

I declined the offer. What possible protection could an eighty-two-year-old Lothario provide? I thanked Doc for the bounteous supper and politely but firmly refused a good-night kiss.

Susannah snoozed all the way home and wasn't any trouble at all. When I got back to the Inn, Billy Dee was the only one still up, and I enlisted his help in carting Susannah off to bed. Then, as a reward, I made a pot of hot chocolate and invited Billy Dee to join me in the parlor.

"Just had me some tea, Miss Yoder. But I'd be glad to sit and shoot the breeze for a spell."

I happily drank Billy Dee's share of the reward. "So how did supper go?" I asked casually. I was dying to know. I also wanted to know who had done the dishes.

Billy chuckled. "You missed a night to remember, Miss Yoder."

"Please . . . Magdalena."

He nodded. "Yep, it was quite something. The Congressman and his missus, and that Delbert guy, they all liked my venison stew. Although the Congressman didn't like the bay leaf. But them other folks! Whew! You'd'a thought I'd drug a skunk in, the way they all scooted down to the other end of the table."

"How about the other dishes? Did you taste them?"

"Some. But you couldn't pay me enough to taste that mess Jeanette served up. Leeks is something that happens to your faucet. Not something you oughta be eating.

"However, that casserole your cook brought over sure hit the spot. Had me two helpings of that."

"What casserole, and what cook?"

"You know, that sort of short woman with the . . . uh . . . the uh . . . the big . . . uh . . ."

"Freni? Freni Hostetler was here?" The department Freni was big in was all too obvious. Susannah and I have often mused that her branch of the family had somehow usurped all the mammary genes in our pool. It may be only a slight exaggeration, but if Susannah and I laid flat on our backs we would make excellent putting greens.

"Yeah," said Billy Dee, "Mrs. Hostetler, that's her name."

"But Freni doesn't even work for me anymore!"

"You fire her?"

"She quit. But with Freni it's all the same. How long was she here for?"

"Just brought the casserole and left. Oh, she did ask where you were. Seemed kinda disappointed you weren't around."

"Well, that's the breaks. How was Linda's salad?"

"Miss Yoder, I mean Magdalena, when I don't know the name of something, I ain't likely to eat it."

"But it was just a salad."

"That's what she said, but there were vegetables in there I ain't never seen before."

Considering the state of Sam's produce, I doubt if even Linda could provide the correct nomenclature. "What about

Lydia's vegetarian curry?" I asked. "That sounded delicious to me."

Billy sighed. "Mrs. Ream is an awfully nice woman, and I didn't want to hurt her feelings, not after she ate my stew and everything, so I tasted her stuff."

"And?"

His expression told me everything. "Couldn't get more than a bite down," he said needlessly. "But I did like the Congressman's beans. And you know what? Even that stuff Joel made wasn't that bad. I ain't never had broiled bananas before, but they're better than they sound. In fact, everyone liked them so much, Joel had to get up and make some more."

"I'll have to get his recipe," I said, although I was pretty sure I wouldn't like them.

Billy Dee and I chatted on a bit more. He confessed that he and Lydia had done the cleanup and all the dishes, but Lydia had made him promise not to give her any credit for the good deed. He also informed me that the next day's plans were pretty much the same as they had been for today. Except, of course, that his team was going to be more vigilant and not let the Congressman's party get away from them. To that end he had already taken the liberty of making up some sandwiches for his group.

"And don't worry about breakfast," said Billy Dee. "We'll each just make our own, if it's all right with you."

"That's perfectly fine. Didn't the Congressman and Delbert have any luck at all today in their hunting?"

"They claim they didn't see a single buck worth taking. But," he lowered his voice conspiratorially, even though there wasn't a soul awake to hear us, "just between you and me, I don't think they even went hunting. Not after deer, anyway. No, sir, I don't think deer's their kind of game."

"Then what is?" What a shame Billy Dee was slipping from the rational category into the absurd.

Billy smiled a wide, Cheshire-cat-like grin. "I aim to find out tomorrow. For sure."

# Chapter Seventeen

For only the second time I can remember, I outslept Susannah. The first time was the morning following my high school prom. No, I was not up all night partying and drinking. I was up all night crying because Mama wouldn't let me go, even though I had been invited by Eldon Shrock, who was a fourth cousin twice removed, and the son of Hernia's mayor. Mama said, and Papa silently agreed, that dancing was the tool the devil used to get young people to fornicate.

"All that rubbing together," Mama had explained, "leads to urges that the body can't control."

"But we'll mostly just be doing the twist," I argued. "We won't even be touching."

"Just the same, Magdalena, vibrations will be jumping back and forth between the two of you, like lightning between two thunderheads."

"But, Mama, the twist is fun. It's no worse than drying off with a towel!" I demonstrated briefly for her benefit.

Mama had blushed and turned quickly away. "Not even with your Papa could I imagine doing such a thing!"

That was it, then. No prom for me, just buckets of tears and eyes that stayed red for a week. Of course, for Susannah, who is ten years younger, everything was different. They were no longer doing the twist. Even the Freddy had flopped by then. At Susannah's prom couples groped and grappled in a dimly lit gym, as thoroughly entwined as a French braid.

By then it was no use asking Mama why Susannah got to go and I didn't. By then the world had changed too much, and Mama with it. At some point in the interim Mama had cut off the long braids she traditionally wore coiled around her head. I was still recovering from the shock of that when she bought a pair of pants to wear for working in the garden. Had Mama lived longer, she might eventually have worn slacks into town and put on lipstick. I still miss Mama terribly, but there is a part of me that is glad she went when she did. Perhaps it's unfair of me to say so, but mothers should look and act like mothers, don't you think?

At any rate, when I awoke that morning, it was because Susannah was shaking me and shouting in my ear.

"Go away," I said. I turned over on my right side and pulled my pillow over my head.

"If you don't come with me, then I'll just go by myself," Susannah shouted. "Shnookums must be absolutely frantic, not knowing where his mama is."

"His mama lives in a kennel in New Jersey, Susannah. Why don't you just write him a letter explaining that?"

"Very funny, Mags. Are you coming with me, or am I driving your car?"

"How did you sleep? Like a lamb?"

"Not bad, although, frankly, I can't remember anything after Doc said he wanted Shnookums to stay the night. Guess I was kind of tired from all the stress."

Poor Susannah, sometimes it's not even fun pulling the wool over her eyes. Grudgingly I got up and drove her over to Doc's. Even before I got out of the car I could hear Shnookums's high-pitched barks through Doc's closed door.

Doc was just setting up to perform gall bladder surgery on a shar-pei when we arrived, but he seemed glad to see us nonetheless. "About time, ladies. This little dog of yours is anxious to get back home."

Susannah looked at me accusingly, and old Doc looked at Shnookums like he might regard a laboratory rat that had bitten him one too many times.

"How is he?" I asked. It doesn't hurt to be hopeful.

"He's as good as can be expected," said Doc noncommittally.

For the moment at least, Susannah's mutt looked like the picture of health to me. As soon as he was released from his cage, Shnookums leaped into Susannah's arms, licked her face a couple of times, and then hopped unceremoniously into the nether reaches of her bosom. I didn't see him for the rest of the day.

When we got back to the house, I suggested to Susannah that we really ought to take advantage of the peace and quiet by doing a thorough dusting and sweeping of all the public rooms.

"But I promised Melvin I would go with him into Breezewood tonight to see a movie," my little sister whined. "I need to wash my hair and get ready."

"Susannah, it's only eleven o'clock in the morning. You'll

have plenty of time to get ready. And which Melvin is this, anyway? Not Melvin Stoltzfus, our acting Chief of Police?" I was mature enough not to make any reference to the bull who hadn't liked being milked, and the consequences of that experience.

"Isn't he dreamy, Mags?"

I rolled my eyes and wrung my hands.

"Well, it's your fault, Magdalena. I hadn't seen him for ages, and then you mentioned seeing him yesterday. So, this morning, while you were sleeping, I called him up and asked him out for coffee, and he invited me out for dinner and a movie instead."

"Why, bite my tongue! But in the meantime, you can help me with the housework, or you're not going to see one thin dime this week." Papa, in his wisdom, left the farm to me with the provision that I see to Susannah's needs until such time as she proved herself competent and productive. If such a day ever comes along, I am morally, if not legally, bound to turn over half the estate to her. So far I haven't come close to worrying about an impending partnership.

Susannah made one of her defiant faces; one that Mama might have found amusing, but not me. "Okay, if you'll just chill for a minute. First let me run upstairs to my own room and find Shnookums his binky. I think it might be under the bed someplace."

I sighed deeply as I acquiesced. A happy Shnookums was a happy Susannah, and if retrieving her dog's binky from under her bed was what it took to get some work out of her, I could live with that. Even though the very notion of a pooch with a pacifier was beyond my comprehension.

"Okay, but make it fast. And don't touch anything in

there. That's a guest room now. We have to respect our guests' privacy."

Susannah headed upstairs while I changed the head on the dust mop. I had just gotten the new cover on when I heard Susannah scream. Even if the house had been full of people, I would have recognized that scream as hers. Hers is an exceptionally high-pitched scream, and while it won't break any glasses, it will curdle milk and put the hens off laying.

Only twice before, not counting Shnookums's bath in the batter, had I heard Susannah scream like that. Once was when she was about eight and stumbled across a still-born calf in the north pasture. The second time was when Reuben Metzer, Hernia's onetime pharmacist and prominent pedophile, exposed himself to her. That happened during a lightning storm on Susannah's tenth birthday. Even though there was an entire room full of little girls already in full scream by then, I immediately picked out Susannah's.

I flung the mop down and bolted up those impossibly steep stairs two at a time. That's when I found Susannah standing in the doorway, staring at the corpse that was clutching Mama's best Dresden Plate quilt.

Like I said before, it was immediately obvious to me that this was a corpse, a victim of murder, not just someone whose time had happened to come during a snooze on Susannah's bed. After I sent Susannah downstairs to look for the borax, I took the phone out into the hallway and called the police. It wasn't until Melvin Stoltzfus picked up the phone that I remembered Chief Myers was out of town.

"I'm sorry, I must have a wrong number," I said. I'm normally not a fast thinker, but I would rather bury a corpse out in the north forty by myself than involve Melvin Stoltzfus.

"Magdalena, is that you? Tell Susannah my mother just called and she wants me to stop by and check out a buzz in her washing machine, so I won't be picking her up until six. Oh, and tell her I'll be wearing my green suit and a green and yellow checkered tie, so she'll know what to wear. Also, do you happen to know if she likes licorice, and if so, does she prefer the bites, the sticks, or the ropes?"

That did it. Melvin Stoltzfus deserved to have a corpse thrown in his lap while his superior was away. Literally, if at all possible. "Put your mother's washing machine and Susannah's licorice on hold, Melvin. I need you to come out to the Inn right away. There's been a murder."

"Quit jumping to conclusions," said Melvin sanctimoniously. "It might just have been an accident. Did you call Alvin Hostetler yet?"

"I'm sending you a compass for Christmas!" I screamed.

"A what?"

"Never mind! I'm not talking about Miss Brown, Melvin. This murder just happened. There's a corpse lying in Susannah's bed."

"Susannah's been murdered?"

"No, not Susannah. One of the guests!"

"Was he her lover?" Melvin sounded as if he were about to burst into tears.

"It's not a he, Melvin. It's a woman."

"Oh my God, that's even worse."

"Get a grip on it, Melvin. They weren't lovers, that's for sure. We needed Susannah's room for one of the guests, so she's been staying with me. How soon are you coming out?"

"I'll be right there. In the meantime don't touch the gun or anything else."

"There is no gun, Melvin."

"What? No gun? But you said it was a murder."

"It is, Melvin. Come out and see for yourself."

"An axe then? Or a club? A shovel maybe?"

"Just a quilt, Melvin. Like I said, come out and see for yourself."

"A quilt? I see, strangulation then. The victim was undoubtedly smothered."

"Somehow I don't think so. Come out and see for yourself."

"Then maybe it's not a murder after all. Are you even sure the so-called victim is dead?"

"Melvin, for Pete's sake, just come on out. And call an ambulance."

"Then she isn't dead?"

"Melvin Stoltzfus!"

Melvin showed up in eight minutes flat, just in front of the ambulance staffed by the volunteer rescue squad. Immediately after calling Melvin, I'd called old Doc Shafer. He showed up on the tail of the ambulance, which goes to show you that not all octogenarians putter along at nine miles an hour. If Melvin hadn't been at the head of the procession, he'd have given old Doc a ticket for sure.

Hernia does have a full-time people doctor, but most folks would rather eat a spoonful of the plague than set eyes on Harold P. Smith III's stethoscope. Young Harold is the epitome of arrogance, and I've heard that most dictionaries revised their definition of that word the year following his birth. Even Susannah says she would rather date a poor lawyer than go out with Harold, so you see what I mean.

Anyway, I'd asked old Doc to come, not for what he might

do for the stiff, but for help in controlling Melvin Stoltzfus. It was one of Doc's patients who kicked Melvin in the head, after all, and it was Doc who undoubtedly patched both of them up. At any rate, everyone in and around Hernia knows and respects old Doc. Doc was my insurance card for getting through the ordeal still sane.

I ushered everyone in and led the way up the stairs to the victim's bedroom. By this time Susannah had returned from the laundry room, without the borax, and was standing by the bed moaning. From within the nether reaches of her blouse Shnookums was following suit with tinny little yowls of his own. I decided that everyone needed a contingent of mourners, even unintentional ones, and to just let them be.

To his professional credit, Melvin appeared to notice the corpse before he noticed Susannah.

"Is this exactly the way you found her?" he asked.

"Naw, she must have gotten up and combed her hair."

"Very funny. Now you and Susannah stand back so I can examine her. This might be rather gruesome."

"No more gruesome than what we can see now," volunteered Doc. "She's been poisoned."

"How the hell do you know that?" snapped Melvin. Quite frankly, I was surprised to hear him swear.

Doc sighed. "Professional instincts, man. Just look at her. It's obvious she died in a great deal of pain, and too quick to call out for help, or to have anyone hear her. Although it's possible, I'd say it's not likely she died of a coronary, given her age."

"How old was she, anyway?" asked Melvin, turning to me.

"Linda is twenty-three."

"Poison then, for sure," said Doc.

"How can you be so sure?" asked Melvin, a little less belligerently.

"Can't be absolutely positive," said Doc, "not until there's been an autopsy. But my best guess is she was poisoned, and at least twelve hours ago. No more than fourteen."

"Twelve hours?" Melvin and I asked at once.

"By the looks of it. Maybe an hour or two more, like I said. Again, the autopsy will take care of that. You sending her right down to the county coroner?"

For a moment Melvin looked wildly around the room. It was obvious that this was his first solo murder, maybe even his first corpse. Perhaps he expected to see a set of instructions flashed against a wall. "Yes, yes, of course. God, I hope he's back by now." He nodded to the two men who had come with the ambulance. They had remained just outside the door and even now seemed reluctant to cross the threshold. It took a couple of sharp words from Melvin to put them into action.

"Be careful of Mama's quilt," I admonished them.

Of course they didn't pay me any attention. They slid the corpse, quilt and all, onto their stretcher. With the very first step he took, one of them stepped on a dragging edge of the quilt, almost pulling the body off with it onto the floor. The quilt pried loose from the clutching hands, but I was sure I heard it rip.

"Now see what you've done!" I said. "I could never make stitches as neat as Mama's." I scooped up the quilt, soiled though it was, and laid it on the bed. That's when I noticed that both on the bed and on the floor, where the quilt had touched down briefly, there was a sprinkling of sunflower seed shells.

"Help me strip the bed," I snapped at Susannah.

"Don't touch a damn thing," said Melvin sharply.

"Why not?"

"Because you might be disturbing evidence, that's why."

Clearly Melvin Stoltzfus watched too much TV. "There aren't any fingerprints on the sheets, Mel." I started to tug at a corner of the bedding.

"Hello, what's this?" asked Melvin. He reached past me and picked something brown and wrinkled-looking from the bed.

"Oh, it's just a sunflower seed shell," I said as nonchalantly as I could. "Linda ate them all the time."

Melvin hiked his pants up over his hipless pelvis with one hand, and with the other practically shoved the stupid shell up my nose. "Trying to hide evidence, were you, Magdalena?"

"Get a grip on it, Melvin," I said as calmly as I could. "If I were trying to hide evidence, wouldn't I have picked up all the shells before you got here? It's not like they're not obvious, after all. There's a blue jillion of them scattered around."

"Ah, but in 'The Purloined Letter,'" said Melvin pompously, "it was obvious too."

Somehow that rang a bell. I thought back and then remembered my eleventh grade English class, a story by Edgar Allan Poe, and something about a letter that was hidden by being placed in plain sight. "Melvin," I said slowly, so that he could read my lips if he needed to, "nobody was trying to hide these sunflower seeds. You can't possibly think that they're poisonous. Can you?"

But possibly Melvin did. He got down on his hands and knees and picked up every one of the little shells and deposited them carefully in a small plastic bag he had brought with him.

# Chapter Eighteen

I waited until Melvin was quite done picking up the shells before I spoke again. "Now may I strip the bed?" I asked reasonably.

"Hell, no!" he nearly exploded. "There still may be more evidence."

"Then you strip it yourself when you're done," I said calmly. I grabbed my still-moaning sister by the shoulders and steered her from the room.

Doc hung back a few minutes, then followed me. We headed downstairs to the parlor. "You know this guest well?" he asked.

"What?"

He gestured back at the room, occupied now only by Melvin. "The corpse, I mean. Did you know the lady well when she was alive?"

I shook my head. "Not really. Just two days. All I know

about her is that she's a vegetarian, and she was here to protest hunting season. Oh, and if the rumors are true, she's the illegitimate daughter of the Congressman."

"What Congressman?"

"Oops, sorry. Garrett Ream."

"That young fart? Anyway, did you know if she was pregnant?"

"Linda? Pregnant?"

"Just a guess, like everything else, but maybe a good one. Of course we'll have to wait until the autopsy comes back."

I trusted Doc enough not even to bother asking why he suspected Linda was pregnant. But I asked him anyway.

Doc laughed, which, at his age, is likely to come out as a cackle. "Intuition, Magdalena. That and the fact that there was a bottle of prenatal vitamins on her night table. Although it's possible, it isn't likely that anyone who wasn't pregnant would be taking them."

"Well, I'll be. Linda pregnant. But if that moron in there sees the pills, he's liable to think she tried to commit suicide."

"By swallowing vitamins?"

I reminded Doc about Melvin's experience with the bull. The more I think about it, the more I'm sure even Melvin Stoltzfus couldn't be that dumb. But then again, you have to be pretty stupid to get a story like that started in the first place.

Old Doc laughed until I thought he would have a coronary. "Unfortunately I don't remember such an episode. But if it did happen, I'm sure Melvin was the one involved. Here," he reached into his pocket and brought out the bottle of vitamins. "Even Melvin can't misinterpret these if he doesn't see them, Magdalena. I nabbed them when the fool was picking up all those sunflower seeds. No point in allowing him to muddy up the waters prematurely."

"But Doc! Isn't that illegal? Swiping evidence?"

"What evidence? No one is going to believe this young lady tried to kill herself by overdosing on a bottle of vitamins. No one, that is, except for young Melvin, who will eventually see the light anyway. So actually, I'm just speeding up the time it will take him to separate the evidence from the incidental. Incidentally, did you happen to notice that the 'do not disturb' sign on the door was still facing out?"

"What 'do not disturb' sign? We don't use those signs around here."

"Yes, you do. Red letters, on a white background. About this big. Saw it myself. Plain as day."

"Well, it isn't ours." I shook Susannah gently. "Did you notice a sign on the door when you first went in there?"

Susannah burst into tears and threw her arms around me. I hate it when someone does that. Even my own sister. My personal space is very important to me. Of course, Susannah didn't notice my discomfort. "I shouldn't have gone in there," she wailed. "I should have started mopping right away, just like you said."

"Nonsense," I said comfortingly. "Your going after Shnookums's binky had nothing to do with Linda's death. Now was there, or was there not, a 'do not disturb' sign hanging on the door?"

Susannah nodded. "There was, Mags. But I swear I knocked first, before opening the door. I knocked real softly, too. I mean, I wouldn't have gone in at all if there had been any kind of an answer."

"Well, how do you like that? A bogus sign. You don't suppose the killer—"

"Put the sign on the door so that no one would discover the young lady's death for a long time, thereby giving him or herself extra time to get away?" old Doc finished for me.

"Does that mean that whenever the guests come back from the woods this afternoon, Mags, the killer will be the only one not to show up?" asked Susannah, with surprising sensibility.

"Yeah, something like that."

"Not necessarily, and probably not at all," said old Doc.

"But you said—"

"I suggested it as a possibility, but I don't think it's at all likely. This killer's too smart to let him or herself be identified by their absence. My guess is that whoever killed this young lady is pretty confident and plans to wait things out."

"But then, why leave the sign?"

"That was just to make sure the poison had a chance to run its course before the victim was discovered. Even if the victim did make some noise, a sign on the door would probably keep people away. At least for a while. Most people are reluctant to investigate even very loud noises when there are 'do not disturb' signs on the doors." I swear the old coot winked at me then.

Susannah laughed, far too bawdily. "You can say that again."

I trust I didn't blush. "Care for anything to eat?"

"Would I ever!" said Doc. He did, after all, live to eat. "But only if you make it from scratch. Who knows what the leftovers in your fridge contain."

I laughed nervously. "Actually, there are no leftovers. At least from last night. Billy Dee, that's one of the guests, said he and Lydia Ream, the Congressman's wife, pitched everything out when the meal was over. They're the ones who did the cleanup," I explained.

Old Doc looked suddenly serious. "That might be your evidence, right there."

"Billy Dee? Lydia Ream? I don't think so. They're the most likable pair in the bunch. I haven't heard a negative word come out of Lydia's mouth, and as for Billy Dee, he gets along with everybody, except maybe with Ms. Parker. But it wasn't Ms. Parker who was poisoned, it was Linda McMahon."

"That's conjecture," said Melvin, entering the room. "We won't know what she died of until we get the lab report back."

"Do we have to wait until then to see if she's even dead?" I know I shouldn't have said it, but I couldn't help myself.

Doc chuckled, Susannah flushed, and Melvin just plain glared. Fortunately for his sake, I couldn't see how Shnookums reacted.

"Well, some things are obvious," I said.

Melvin drew himself up to his full height, which diminished the praying mantis image but made him look like a wide-eyed child playing grown-up. "When you assume," he intoned, "you make an *ass* out of *u* and *me*."

"I do not allow obscene language in this house, Mr. Stoltzfus."

"For chrissakes, Magdalena, he was only trying to make a point," said my much misguided sister.

"Susannah Yoder! Mama would . . ."

"Entwhistle, Mags, and leave Mama out of this. What Melvin said is true. You're always jumping to conclusions. And another thing, you're always judging people. Always coming down on them with your own rigid standards. Like you're the only one who's right. Like what's right for you has to be what's right for everyone else. You're always critical, you know? You're too hard on people, Mags. Give us a break sometimes."

Well, I didn't have to just sit there and take that. "Doc, about lunch, why don't we convene to the kitchen, where we're not unwanted?"

"Good idea," said Doc.

"Hey, we get to eat too," said Susannah.

"Fine, then you go to the kitchen and make lunch."

"You want to stay for lunch, honey?" Susannah asked Melvin. Just when their relationship had had time to blossom to the honey stage was beyond me.

"Well," drawled Melvin, "I do need to stay and question the suspects when they return. How about if you and I order in pizza?"

"Dreamy," drooled Susannah.

I knew for a fact that poor Mama was going to get a lot of exercise that day. Hernia does not have a pizza parlor, and whatever it was Susannah and Melvin planned to do in Mama's parlor had little, if anything, to do with lunch.

"Remember this is a Christian house, Susannah," I admonished her futilely.

My sister feigned shock. "There you go again, Mags. Always jumping to conclusions."

"At least it's a decent form of exercise."

"Too bad you can't compare the two," she countered cruelly.

I didn't subject myself to any more of that. Instead I took my frustration out on fixing Doc the best lunch he'd had in seventeen years. At least that's what he said about it. We barricaded ourselves in the kitchen and pigged out like we were teenagers.

We were just finishing up the last of the cherry cobbler, with black cherry ice cream, when Billy Dee came bursting into the kitchen. "What the hell is going on, Miss Yoder, and just who the hell is that in the parlor?"

Perhaps it was because I was satiated, or maybe because I realized it was pointless, but I ignored Billy Dee's profanity. "You do know that Linda's dead?"

Billy Dee sat down heavily on one of the kitchen stools. "That's what that fellow in there says. Is it true? My God, he's got Jeanette hysterical with his accusations."

"Linda is dead," I said gently. "That's for sure. Susannah found her. I saw for myself. It was awful. And as for that guy in there, he's with the police. I had to call him."

Billy Dee shook his head in apparent bewilderment. "I just can't believe it. There weren't a thing wrong with her last night. And that fellow says there might have been foul play. Do you think there was?"

I looked over at Doc.

"Can't say for sure," he said, "but it would appear so. Looked like poisoning to me."

Billy Dee rubbed his hands through his still-thick, only slightly graying hair. "It's just so damn hard to believe. Who would do such a thing?"

"Your guess has got to be better than ours," I said.

"What is that supposed to mean?"

"Well, you did know Linda better, much better, than I. You're much more likely to know why someone would want her dead."

"Linda? Not a damn clue! Jeanette, yes, but not Linda. Hell, I've been tempted to kill Jeanette myself, but I don't know nobody that's got a thing against Linda."

"Well, maybe it was an accident then," I suggested.

Old Doc licked the foam of melted ice cream off his lips. "Could be. If she'd eaten toadstools or something. But from what's available on Sam Yoder's shelves, you'd have to be a wizard to put together something that toxic."

"I don't know about that. Sam sells some weird produce, Doc."

Billy Dee didn't appear to be listening. "It's my fault," I thought I heard him mutter.

"What did you say?"

"I might have been able to save her, Miss Yoder."

"How so?"

He shook his head from side to side. "Last night, after I said good night to you, I went up to see if Linda was still awake. I wanted to see if she could talk some sense into Jeanette. I thought maybe Linda could convince Jeanette to hold a simple press conference and call this whole stalking thing off. Because it really ain't nothing more than harassment. It doesn't accomplish anything."

"Harassment seems to be Jeanette's specialty. But go on, how could you have saved Linda?"

Billy slapped his leg hard with the palm of his hand, as if punishing himself. "That damned sign was already on the door then, so I didn't even bother to knock. But I should have suspected something was fishy. There ain't no sign like that in my room, so it should have been a clue."

"Naw," said Doc wisely, "that doesn't mean anything. Lots of folks travel with their own 'do not disturb' signs. You know what I mean?" He winked lasciviously, presumably at me again.

"I wouldn't know about that, Doc."

Just then Joel stuck his head in the room. From where I sat, he looked like he had been crying. "The officer wants to see you, Billy Dee," he said.

Billy Dee got up and walked off slowly. Joel took his place on the stool.

"This is Doc Shafer," I said by way of introduction. "And this is Joel Teitlebaum from Philadelphia." I don't know where my manners had gone when it was time to introduce Billy Dee.

"I'm the animal kind of doc, not the human kind," said my friend modestly.

Joel couldn't have cared less. "It's all my fault," he practically wailed. At this range it was obvious he had been crying.

"Let me see," I pretended to muse, "you saw the 'do not disturb' sign hanging on Linda's door, and you didn't disturb her, when doing so might have saved her life?"

Joel stopped a silent sob in mid-sniffle and regarded me with surprise. "How did you know?"

"Intuition. But never mind that. Tell me, how's Jeanette holding up? After all, she is Linda's mother." I tactfully omitted saying that I personally thought Jeanette was as capable of feeling love as was a turnip.

Young Joel's mouth fell open about as wide as mine did the day I got home from school early and discovered Mama and Papa having sex. "She's what? What did you say?"

"I simply stated that Jeanette is, or should I say, was, Linda's mother. Surely you knew that."

"I just can't believe that. I mean, how do you know?"

I shrugged. "I guess someone told me. Sorry, I thought it was common knowledge. But anyway, how is Jeanette doing?"

Joel pulled a handkerchief from his pocket, and in so doing spilled a few sunflower seeds on my kitchen floor. "Jeanette is very upset, of course. After all, they were close, even if they were just friends. Which, of course, I guess they weren't, since they happen to be mother and daughter."

"They seemed close," I conceded. "Then again, all you A.P.E.S. members seem close, which doesn't leave much room for suspects, does it? Unless the murderer is one of the Congressman's party?"

I thought I saw Joel squirm, but he might just have been shifting slightly on his stool. Those stools are rather hard and uncomfortable. "Why in the world would any of the Congressman's party have it in for Linda?" he asked wide-eyed. "She never even saw them before Sunday night."

"Beats me. But speaking of which, did you guys catch up with them in the woods today?"

Joel's long sculptor's fingers picked aimlessly at a sunflower seed that was stuck to his handkerchief. "If you ask me, they didn't even go hunting today. We drove by every public access to state game lands in the county and didn't see a sign of their car. They're obviously not playing fair. This whole thing isn't fair. Linda never hurt a fly, and now she's dead. The Congressman, on the other hand, is a sleaze, and he gets away with everything. Life just isn't fair."

"Life is never fair, Joel. Those times when it seems like it, it's just coincidence."

"Life sucks," said old Doc succinctly. "I ought to know. I've lived enough of it to be something of an expert on the subject."

"But, my God, this is too much," sobbed Joel. He buried his face in the handkerchief with the sunflower seed still clinging to it. "Linda didn't deserve to die. And I know you don't like her, Miss Yoder, but Jeanette didn't deserve to lose a daughter, either. She must be in terrible pain."

I got up and headed for the parlor. I had to see for myself how Jeanette was doing. Much to my surprise, Melvin didn't seem to mind when I slipped into the room. Perhaps he didn't even notice.

But Jeanette did. She was sitting on a footstool, weeping quietly in front of the fireplace. Billy Dee was down on one knee with an arm around her, and on the other side Susannah was doing the same. Melvin was standing a few feet to Susannah's left, seemingly staring off into space. Together, they looked like a Norman Rockwell painting that might have been titled "Grief." Except for Jeanette, nobody seemed to notice my entering the room. The second I slipped in, she rose to her feet and pointed a finger in my direction.

"There she is!" she screamed. "There's the woman who killed my little girl!"

For a split second I thought of slipping out again, but of course it was too late. With that one accusation Jeanette Parker had undoubtedly sent Mama spinning so fast in her grave that the heat she generated might compel God to send her to the other place. For Mama's sake I had to stay and sort things out.

# Chapter Nineteen

Melvin Stoltzfus snapped to attention. "What did you say?"

"She didn't say anything," I ventured. "She screamed."

Jeanette's finger, which was still pointing at me, vibrated on the end of her hand like that obscene thing I once saw Susannah hide away. "Murderess! There's the woman who killed my little girl."

Melvin flashed me a look that would have been a smirk on someone with lips. "Why do you say that?"

Jeanette sat down again. "She's the one who bought the food that poisoned my little girl. She's the one who asked us all to cook something for that disastrous meal. And then she didn't even stay to eat it. Doesn't that prove it?"

"Let's say it raises some questions," said Melvin. Frankly, I was surprised at his restraint. I would have thought the praying mantis would have been glad for any excuse to pounce on me.

"Yeah, like the fact that Susannah didn't stay to eat it

either. In fact, it was Susannah's fault we had to skip out to begin with."

"Thanks a lot, Mags!" sang out Susannah. "Melvin, it's not just because she's my sister, but I really don't think Magdalena would do such a thing."

For once I was proud of my baby sister.

"And why not?" asked Melvin. It was obvious he respected Susannah's opinions.

"Well, for one thing, Magdalena doesn't even kill spiders. And for another thing, that's not like her at all. My sister is just too . . . too . . ."

"Too dull?" I asked. "How about the fact that I don't have a motive?"

"Oh, well, there is that, too," Susannah admitted.

"But speaking of motive," I continued, "you might find one or two amongst Congressman Ream's party."

Jeanette seemed to shift on her stool, just like Joel had.

"How's that?" asked Melvin.

I couldn't bring myself to look at Jeanette as I spoke, so I focused on a spot above the fireplace mantel where Mama had hung a painting of "Jesus Knocking at the Door." The painting was gone now, and in its place hung a brightly colored Pennsylvania Dutch hex sign. It seemed like an appropriate place to look. I began to explain slowly.

"Well, it has been brought to my attention that the Congressman is the victim's biological father."

Jeanette gasped but said nothing.

"Go on," said Melvin.

"So, you see the connection, don't you? Maybe the Congressman wanted Linda out of the way for political reasons, especially since he may well decide to run for President, if he gets as far as the Senate. An illegitimate daughter," I swallowed hard, "might be too much political baggage for even Garrett Ream to carry."

"Now wait just one cotton-picking minute," said Billy Dee. "Who told you that?"

"If you don't believe the Congressman is Linda's father, just ask Ms. Parker."

"That's not what I mean," said Billy Dee impatiently. "Who told you the Congressman has plans for national office?"

I hope Susannah was proud of me, because I didn't even glance in her direction. "I have my sources. And anyway that's not the issue. The issue is that Garrett Ream has a motive."

"Hardly," said Melvin. "Nobody's likely to kill his own daughter just to be President. The issue is the daughter, not whether she's alive or dead."

I must admit he had me there. "Well, what about Mrs. Ream?" As much as I liked the woman, it was better her skin than mine.

"What about her?"

"Well," I fumbled, "maybe she couldn't stand to be confronted with her husband's indiscretion."

Jeanette stood up and jabbed her finger in my direction again. "Linda was not the result of some indiscretion. Garrett and I were lovers. True lovers. We loved each other passionately, and long before he met Ms. High and Mighty."

"Well, that certainly isn't our business, is it? I mean, about you and the Congressman being 'true lovers.' That sort of thing."

"Apparently that 'sort of thing' has never been your business, so why don't you just butt the hell out?"

"Ladies, ladies," chided Billy Dee gently, "like the man says, we need to stick to the issue."

"Well, what about Delbert James?" asked Susannah helpfully. Although she's my own sister, sometimes it seems like Susannah's bulb is so dim even an owl couldn't read by it.

"What about him?" Melvin and I asked together.

Susannah sat gaping silently at us like a hen who has seen the hawk but doesn't know in which direction to run.

"Actually, she might have a point," said Billy Dee gallantly. "Delbert James might have done it. In fact, any of us might have done it, inadvertently."

"You mean that possibly the intended victim was someone other than Linda McMahon?" Melvin seemed to come alive with this new realm of possibilities.

"Yeah, that's what I mean. Now take this Delbert guy, I don't hardly know him, but him and the Congressman are too tight, if you ask me. Like maybe one's got something on the other. Maybe he was trying to poison the Congressman, or the other way around, and Linda ate whatever it was by mistake."

"Or maybe Delbert and the Congressman are gay and Mrs. Ream was trying to poison Delbert," suggested Susannah. Honestly, she should have left well enough alone.

"Don't be such a stupid twit," said Jeanette. "Garrett is far from gay."

Nobody speaks to my sister like that, except for me. "Well, then, maybe you were trying to poison Garrett because he dumped you, and you accidentally poisoned your own daughter."

"Nobody dumped me," Jeanette practically shrieked.

I didn't flinch. "Or maybe you were trying to poison Lydia Ream because you were jealous of her."

"Why the hell should I be jealous of that insipid, bourgeois sheep? Garrett and I split up twenty-three years ago."

In order not to escalate the hostilities, I suppressed a chuckle. If Lydia Ream was bourgeois, then so was Princess Di. "May I go now?"

I had addressed the question to Melvin Stoltzfus, but Jeanette Parker answered. "By all means, do. Nobody asked you to come in here to begin with."

"I do own this place," I reminded her.

"But not for long, I promise you that. I plan to sue you for everything you've got, Ms. Yoder. You can expect to hear from my lawyers as soon as I get home."

"Ha! Not if someone else beats you to it," I said. "You can't squeeze blood from a stone." I'd rather have the mousy Miss Brown's estate wring me dry than that loud-mouth Jeanette.

"The Inn is entirely in my sister's name," Susannah piped up.

"The rats are jumping ship now, are they?" I asked her.

"Leave Shnookums out of this!"

I glared at everyone in the room, including Billy Dee, who hadn't offered anything like the support I had hoped for, and left the parlor. I grabbed my coat from the front closet by the desk and went out the front door and around the house to feed the chickens and gather eggs.

That Mose had already attended to them was irrelevant. I have always found surrounding myself with chickens to be therapeutic. There is something about their squawking and squabbling that empowers me, especially if it is I who have generated the hee-cack. Chickens have many human characteristics, if you stop to think about it. They can be "mad as a wet hen," "gabby old hens," "cocky," have "something to crow about," and, of course, just plain old "chicken." I suppose your average therapist would have a field day with this, but I enjoy being a Brobdingnagian in their Lilliputian world. Chickens fear and respect me, which is more than I can say for anything else in this world.

As usual, the chickens were flapping and squawking out of my way as I reached into their nest boxes to get out the eggs. In most instances hens will stay put and sometimes even peck the hand that tries to pluck their eggs, but not my darlings. Even the dumbest of them learned early in the game that I will goose any hen who doesn't vacate her box immediately.

I had just managed to intimidate Pertelote, the boldest of my hens, into leaving her nest, when I heard the most awful disturbance behind me. Foxes might be historically infamous for raiding henhouses, but in Hernia it's coons, nine times out of ten. And lately, raccoons have gotten bolder and bolder and are as likely to make a foray into fowldom in broad day-light as they are at night. If I wasn't a pacifist by heritage, I would buy a gun and blow those masked bandits to kingdom come.

I whirled around, half-expecting to see a raccoon. "Lydia!"

"Hello, Magdalena."

"What on earth are you doing here?" Even in her hunting clothes Lydia Ream looked far too elegant to grace the inside of a henhouse.

"Magdalena, I need to talk to you." Lydia advanced a few tentative steps.

"Don't worry, those hens are just as afraid of you as you are of them."

Lydia pointed down at her shoes. "It's not them I'm afraid of."

"Right. Why don't we step outside into my office?"

She continued to weave her way across the floor to me. "No, I'd rather talk in here."

"Suit yourself then." After all, if a Senator's daughter and Congressman's wife, not to mention a potential First Lady, wanted to chat with me in a chicken coop, who was I to object?

"We just got in," said Lydia. "No sooner had we walked through the front door than this monstrous little man pounced on us and said Linda was dead. Said she was poisoned. He also said everyone here at the Inn is a suspect, at least until they get back the coroner's report. Is that true?"

"That monstrous little man is Melvin Stoltzfus. And, yes, Linda is dead. Susannah found her in bed late this morning. As for all of us being suspects, some of us are less so than others."

Lydia shook her head. "What a tragedy. Linda was so young. Who could have done such a terrible thing? And that man—that Mellwood somebody—doesn't seem to possess an ounce of sensitivity. Garrett and Delbert are in there talking to him right now, but I had to find you right away."

"Praying mantises eat their mates," I said simply.

"What?"

"Never mind. How did you know where to find me?"

"Your sister told me. She said you find chickens comforting." Lydia smiled as if she approved. "Magdalena, the reason I need to talk to you is because you are such a sensible woman. Why, just look, even your shoes are sensible."

Lydia paused while I glanced down at my feet. When Susannah says that I wear sensible shoes, she means it as an insult.

"And, so," continued Lydia smoothly, "I was hoping that you might help extricate us from a delicate problem."

"Who is us, and what's the problem?" The last time I was asked that question was when Susannah was still a teenager. She had wanted me to buy condoms for her boyfriend, Noah Miller. Of course I told her "no," and then I told Noah to keep his pecker in his pants where it belonged.

Lydia smiled, and as much as I liked her, I could still tell it was a political smile. "Well, I guess by 'us' I meant the Congressman. You see, Magdalena, my husband has been fighting a slight problem with substance abuse."

"Are such problems ever slight?"

She smiled again, this time patiently. "What I mean is that Garrett can still function. You know, carry on with his duties. But he does have a problem, I'm not denying that."

"I see."

"But I'm afraid you don't." Lydia reached out and grabbed my sleeve with a perfectly manicured hand. "We aren't here as hunters this week, Magdalena. In fact, hunting is the farthest thing from our minds."

"Then why are you here? The food?" That was supposed to have been a little joke.

Lydia didn't even smile. "We're here scouting out a new rehabilitation clinic in the Laurel Mountains. The Grossinger-Beechman Clinic. Have you heard of it?"

I nodded. There had been a big stink about it in the Hernia *Weekly Herald*. Something about drug-crazed rock stars invading our peaceful domain to get their heads screwed on straight at the risk of our homes and hearths. Since I hadn't recognized any of the names, and it was all privately funded, I hadn't paid the matter any attention.

"The first day we were here, Monday, Garrett did go hunting, but just as a ruse to get them off his scent. Today, however, we headed straight for the clinic, where he had his interview. Tomorrow, he had planned to commit himself for a three-week stint."

"And you planned to keep all this a secret?"

"From the press, surely. And from that awful woman, Jeanette Parker, who is worse than the press. That woman has been relentless in her persecution of Garrett ever since he took office. She is obsessed with her crusade to do him in politically."

"And that awful woman, of course, just happens to be your husband's ex-lover."

I did not mean to be cruel. Nonetheless, Lydia's mouth fell open like a trapdoor with a sprung lever. "You know about that?"

"The walls have ears, Lydia, or in this case make it the floorboards. Take it from an experienced innkeeper, whenever you're not in your own home, you're in public." Boy, did I know the truth of that statement. Susannah and I had been living in a fishbowl, albeit of my own making, for ten years now.

Lydia didn't seem to appreciate my advice. "What else did you hear?"

"I beg your pardon?"

"What else did you hear through those floorboards, Magdalena?" Even classy people can sound nasty if they try hard enough.

"Well, you needn't worry about that!" I had begun to get huffy myself. "Susannah has oiled all the bedsprings."

Lydia laughed then, perhaps with relief. "Well, I guess I did get carried away there for a moment. Anyway, what I came to ask you, Magdalena, was for help in keeping this matter a private one."

"I see," I said, although actually I didn't. "How on earth can I help in that regard?"

Lydia rubbed the sole of one of her expensive shoes against a clump of straw. "Well, you are well-known in the community here, and I imagine you exert a considerable amount of local influence. Perhaps you can talk this young officer, whom you seem already to know, into not disclosing publicly where Garrett was today or what his plans are. You know, use some of that influence. After all, it has nothing to do with young Linda, and revealing it could be disastrous to his career."

It was my turn to laugh. "Me? Influence Melvin Stoltzfus? I can't even get my sister to pick up her dirty underwear. But speaking of which, Susannah is the one you should be talking to. If anyone can influence Melvin, she can."

Lydia seemed taken aback. "Well, then," she said at last, "could you talk to your sister for me? This is a difficult subject for me to talk about, as you might imagine, and I haven't really gotten a chance to know your sister."

I studied Lydia Ream for a moment. I savored that moment. There is something uniquely satisfying about having a rich, elegant, well-bred socialite beg for one's help in a chicken coop. "Okay, I'll talk to Susannah, but I doubt if it will do any good. If Melvin Stoltzfus has already made up his mind about something, it simply won't be possible for anyone, even Susannah, to change it."

"But you'll have her try?"

"She'll try, but like I said, don't count on his being reasonable. He was kicked in the head by a bull, you know."

"Pardon me?"

"Oh, nothing, just a joke. Now, unless you have any other requests, it's about time we got out of here. Chickens carry fleas, you know, and when it's cold like this, the fleas in the straw on the floor hop up on humans seeking warmth."

Lydia exited rapidly, and I followed. She might have been fleeing the fleas, but I was feeling ravenous again. Stress always does that to me. Fortunately, I still have the metabolism rate of a teenager, otherwise I'd be as big as Aunt Agnes was in her prime. When my mother's sister died, they buried her in the packing crate her Frigidaire had come in. Even then, I'm told, they had to band the box with metal straps to keep her from popping out.

"Have lunch yet?" I called out after Lydia.

She must not have heard me, because she didn't even answer. I can't blame her, though, even if she did. Women in Lydia's league don't often face flea infestation from henhouses. Even their dogs are dipped more often than soft-serve cones at Neubrander's Dairy Bar.

As for me, all I could think of then was food. Fleas, and come to think of it, praying mantises like Melvin Stoltzfus, would just have to wait until after I'd had something else to eat. With any luck I would find Joel still in the kitchen and convince him to whip me up some of his famous broiled bananas. Since they were the only dish that everyone had eaten the night before, and in fact had even had an encore, they must have been good. I couldn't wait to taste this interesting concoction.

# Chapter Twenty

## JOEL TEITLEBAUM'S
## FAMOUS BROILED BANANA RECIPE

Several large, unripe bananas
An ample supply of lemon juice
Copious amounts of brown sugar
A generous amount of cinnamon
An inquiring mind

Butter or otherwise grease an ovenproof dish. Peel and slice the bananas into quarters. Arrange seed-side up in the dish. Splash with lemon juice. Heap with brown sugar. Sprinkle with cinnamon.

Broil in the oven, about six inches from the heating element, until the brown sugar begins to melt and caramelize (about 3 to 5 minutes). Spoon lemon juice–sugar syrup mixture from the pan over the bananas and serve hot.

# Chapter Twenty-one

Unfortunately Joel was not in the kitchen. Doc still was, however, and he was happily making himself a plate full of fried baloney and ketchup sandwiches. He asked me to join him, and of course I accepted.

"Want some fresh eggs to go with that?" I asked. Pertelote's issue was still warm to the touch.

Doc said he would, and I got out another pan and fried up Pertelote's egg and three others. I like my eggs greasy, slightly runny, and almost black with pepper. Doc likes them the same way.

"Called Ed Houlihan, while you were out," said Doc casually. Mr. Houlihan was the county coroner, a trained pathologist, and a contemporary of Doc's. They'd started in medical school together, before Doc switched over to veterinary medicine. Ed was the antithesis of Melvin Stoltzfus in that he had been at his job since back in the days when God was still young. As far as I knew no one had ever run against Ed in the elections, and I don't suppose they ever will. County coroner is not a glamorous job in these parts. That probably explains why Ed can afford to take four-day holiday weekends.

"Ed's back finally? The autopsies are done already?"

Doc waved his spatula in annoyance. "You young people have no concept of patience. You can't even butcher a chicken that fast. I just wanted to tell you that Ed said he'd give me a call when the results are in."

"When do you think that will be?"

"You're always in a hurry, Magdalena." He waved the spatula again. "Ed has to send a few samples from each of them down to Harrisburg, and you know how slow those boys are."

"I see." If they were anywhere near as slow as the boys in the Bureau of Motor Vehicles, neither Doc nor I stood a very good chance of living long enough for the results to come back.

"But in the meantime, it's pretty clear that both women died of respiratory failure. Miss Brown was apparently dead before her fall." Doc let that sink in for a moment.

My Stoltzfus blood fought valiantly to keep me in the dark, but then the light broke through. "You mean she was murdered?" I cried joyfully. The PennDutch was mine again; Jeanette's suit didn't stand a chance.

Doc nodded. "It would appear so. But it's not conclusive yet. Her falling down the stairs might have been the result of her dying, but that doesn't automatically mean she was murdered. She may have stopped breathing for a number of other reasons."

"And Linda? You said she died of respiratory failure as well. So then it wasn't poison?"

Doc gave me a look that would have curdled buttermilk,

had there been any out in the open. "I didn't say it wasn't poison. Respiratory failure is often the cause of death from fast-acting poisons. Both plant and animal poisons."

"Animal poisons? What kind?"

"Snakes, mainly. Some marine life as well."

"Spiders?"

Instead of getting angry again, Doc laughed. "Give it a rest, Magdalena. It wasn't a spider that did Linda in. Ed could tell that much already."

I breathed a sigh of relief. It's not that I didn't care about Linda, but I cared even more about avoiding a lawsuit for negligent housekeeping, or whatever it was they would have charged me with, had it been a spider. That is, had the spider in question been a homegrown one and not some fancy imported variety.

"If it's any comfort," said Doc needlessly, "that young lady died about as quickly as it's possible to die."

I flashed up a picture of young Linda, lying on Susannah's bed and clutching one of Mama's quilts. "She might have died fast, but it sure wasn't painless. I'd just as soon go in my sleep."

"Wouldn't we all."

I was about to say something witty about the way old Doc would undoubtedly depart the Earth, but my mind flitted back to the scene I'd just conjured up. There was something definitely wrong with it. Something was very much out of place, but I couldn't seem to hold the scene in my mind long enough to figure it out.

"A penny for your thoughts," said Doc gently.

"They aren't worth much right now, that's for sure. I've been thinking about seeing Linda lying there on Susannah's bed, and something's just not right."

Doc smiled. "Besides the fact that she was dead?"

"Yes, besides that."

Just then Freni came into the kitchen through the back door. She seemed surprised to find anyone there, especially Doc.

"Afternoon, Freni," said Doc with what was undoubtedly forced joviality.

Freni jerked her head in acknowledgment. She was no more fond of old Doc than he was of her. The Doc/Freni feud, I'm told, goes back even to before I was born. I'm not even sure what it's about, but I am sure it's as clear as crystal in both their minds. Neither of them forgets anything, and both of them seem to have a genuine need to be generally disliked. Freni more so than Doc. Doc at least has Ed Houlihan and a few other old cronies to pal around with. Freni, now that Mama's gone, has only Mose and me.

"Thanks for bringing the casserole over last night," I practically sang out. I'm all for diverting confrontations.

"No problem, Magdalena, except, of course, that you weren't here."

"Sorry, Freni, but you did hear what happened to Shnookums."

"Grown men should have more important things to do than treating English dogs," said Freni, looking somewhere just past Doc's ear. "Anyway, Magdalena, I'm here to start supper. Same old crowd, I suppose." Freni opened the fridge and began rummaging around.

"You suppose right, Freni. Well, sort of, anyway. One of them's dead."

Her voice showed no sign of surprise. "And which one is that?"

"The young woman. Linda was her name."

"A shame," said Freni simply.

She started busying herself with supper preparations without clearing anything with me first, including her employment
status. From the way she acted, Freni knew exactly what she
planned to cook, and that was that. By the looks of what she
had lined up on the table, Jeanette and Joel were simply going
to be out of luck. Freni, it was clear, had come back with a
vengeance.

Doc and I ate our second lunch in respectful silence. We
were very careful, however, to chew our food slowly, so it
should have been obvious, even to Freni, that we were not at
all intimidated by her presence.

When we were quite done, I said good-bye to Doc, who
had a four-o'clock appointment to spay the Methodist minis-
ter's Doberman. Then, after a quick prayer and a couple of
deep breaths, I worked up enough nerve to sneak back into
the parlor. The game was essentially still the same, except for
the addition of a few more players.

"Then where were you, if you weren't hunting?" Melvin
was asking the Congressman. Incidentally, Melvin used the
same tone of voice with the Congressman as he did with me. I
took some comfort in that.

The Congressman, on the other hand, did not seem to
possess the bottomless font of patience that I am so famous for.
"Look here, kid," said Garrett, "either I'm a suspect or I'm not.
If I'm not, then my whereabouts today are none of your damn
business. And you can be damn sure the Governor's going to
hear about this. Delbert, give Paul a ring as soon as this cretin
lets us go."

Perhaps I did feel just a wee bit sorry for Melvin. After all, he was a local boy, and probably really was some kind of kin if I looked hard enough. "Pardon me," I interjected, "but there's a phone call for you, Melvin. In the kitchen."

Melvin looked desperately grateful, although I fully expected him to chew me out later for having addressed him by his first name. At any rate, he followed me like a puppy dog into the kitchen. It was clear he wasn't actually expecting there to be a call waiting for him, and I thought briefly, and then discarded the notion, about revising my opinion of his intelligence.

"Melvin, dear," I began, "there's something important I should tell you." "Dear," in case it's escaped your notice, is a form of address reserved exclusively for use by middle-aged women when they want to be condescending. Although usually this form of condescension is employed by sales clerks, we hoi polloi have rightful access to it as well. Of course, as we all know, at about age fifty-five we need to substitute the word "honey" for "dear" when we stoop to condescend. The principle remains the same, however.

As a truly acculturated man under forty, Melvin responded much better to condescension than he ever had to confrontation. "Yes, Miss Yoder?"

I told Melvin about Lydia's conversation with me in the henhouse. By the time I was through, Melvin Stoltzfus looked like he was about ready to cry. He was clearly out of his league. "What do you think I should do, Miss Yoder?"

"Pray more," said Freni. I'm sure she meant it.

"Have you considered calling in the big boys?" I hadn't meant to be insulting. "What I mean is, can't you just turn this over to the county? You know, call the Sheriff in on it."

Melvin shook his head, probably to hide the fact that he

was blinking. Given the size of Melvin's eyes, he wasn't fooling anyone. "Jeff, I mean the Chief, put me in charge while he's away. I'm supposed to handle everything that comes up within this jurisdiction. He's counting on me, Miss Yoder. I'm supposed to follow normal procedure."

"Well, then, what is normal procedure in this case?"

It wouldn't have surprised me if Melvin had consulted a handbook, but he didn't. "I am authorized to detain everyone who was on or had access to these premises, for the next twenty-four hours, or until the coroner's report is returned. At which time I must—"

"Freni!" My kinswoman and sometime cook was trying to sneak out the back door. What with supper just hours away, I couldn't afford to let that happen.

"I'm just going out to get some eggs," said Freni haltingly. Most Amish women are terrible liars.

I smiled. "No need to, dear. I just collected them all a half hour ago."

Freni's face turned a nice, deep red, which actually went quite well with her blue gingham dress. "W-w-well," she stammered, "t-this recipe requires a lot of eggs. I'm going to need some more. Maybe some have been laid since then."

Maliciously I opened the fridge door. "Do you need more than four dozen?"

"I was only here for ten minutes last night," said Freni. "All I did was bring a casserole. And this is the thanks I get? Being accused of murder?"

"No one's accused you of anything," Melvin tried to explain, but Freni would have none of it.

"Your grandmother and I are cousins," she said. I'm sure she meant the term loosely. "But we're more like sisters. And your grandfather and I are cousins on the Bontrager side. I've known you all your life, Melvin, long before that bull kicked you in the head, and you have the nerve to accuse me of murder?"

"Freni!" This time it was Mose. I hadn't seen him come in, so compelling was Freni's performance.

I let Mose try and calm Freni down while I attempted to do the same with Melvin. That comment about having been kicked in the head clearly seemed to have upset him. Perhaps there was truth to the rumor. Undoubtedly Melvin had heard it before.

"Don't pay any attention to what she said, Melvin. Freni Hostetler is as high-strung as a telephone pole on Mars. She speaks first and thinks later. But deep inside she's a pussycat."

"Cats have claws, Miss Yoder. Anyway, what do you think I should do now?"

"Detain all the guests," I advised, "but let Freni go home for the night when she's done here. It's not like we don't know where to find her. What's she going to do, make a mad dash for the Maryland border in her buggy?"

Much to my surprise, Melvin accepted my advice. He told everyone except Freni that no charges had been levied yet but that none of them was to leave the township of Hernia until the coroner's report came in. I was surprised again when virtually no one complained about having to spend another night at the Inn. Perhaps it was because they were all paid up through the end of the week. At any rate, even the Congressman seemed to have calmed down a bit.

To Freni, Melvin said not another word. The Hostetler farm, incidentally, lies just over the township boundary, a fact undoubtedly known to Melvin. I think Freni should have been grateful that he seemed to have dropped the matter, but of course she wasn't. She didn't even bother to put her supper makings back into the fridge before she left.

"I will not be spoken to like that by Sarah Stoltzfus's grandson, Magdalena. Your mama would turn over in her grave if she knew that little Melvin had accused me of murder."

"Leave Mama out of it, Freni!"

"And don't you use that tone of voice on me, Magdalena. I won't stand here and take that."

"Then go home, Freni."

"Good. I will. I quit!"

"Until next time, Freni."

Fortunately, at that point Mose managed to shuffle his wife out the door. Needless to say, I felt sorry for him. He was forever having to extricate his wife from unpleasant situations —situations caused by distinctively un-Amish behavior on her part. Freni needed either to see a therapist or to seriously consider becoming a Baptist. A pacifist, she was not.

I looked at the mess Freni had left spread out on the table. Whatever it was she had planned for supper, it was beyond me. Something with pig's knuckles and spiced apple rings, no doubt, but certainly not a menu that would garner even the majority approval of our guests.

"What can I make for supper that everyone will like?" I asked myself. Several times. It is a well-known fact that talking to one's self is proof of high intelligence.

The very intelligent, of course, talk back to themselves. "Why bother to even try," I heard myself eventually answer.

"Just make them tomato soup and grilled peanut butter sandwiches. Given the circumstances, they should be happy to get anything."

And for the most part, they were.

# Chapter Twenty-two

Jeanette didn't even come down to supper. I can't say as I blamed her. When Mama and Papa died, I went about a week without eating. Anyway, I took a bowl of soup and a grilled peanut butter sandwich up to her when supper was over.

"Thanks," was all she said.

I couldn't believe it. I'd expected at least one heavy-duty criticism, maybe even a repeated accusation, but such was not the case. "Let me know if you need anything," I offered. I meant it.

"Thanks," she said again.

I went back downstairs feeling more than a little uneasy. This was not the same Jeanette who had flung accusations at me in the parlor just hours before. This woman was almost a stranger.

Her subdued responses aside, there was something very different about the woman. I couldn't pinpoint what it was exactly, but I thought it might even have something to do with

the way she looked. The intense energy, albeit negative, that
Jeanette usually projected, was curiously absent. This Jeanette
looked about as perky as I must look when I wake up from a
too long nap.

Of course I didn't dwell on Jeanette. She was a big girl,
after all. And anyway I had problems of my own to contend
with.

"How dare you?" screamed Susannah when I got back to
the kitchen.

"How dare I what?"

"Melvin just called, and he's canceling our date tonight
altogether."

"Somebody should be grateful."

"What's that supposed to mean? Magdalena, this is all your
fault. If you hadn't gone and opened your big yap, I'd be in
Breezewood right now, buying popcorn for the movie."

"Did you wash the quilt and Linda's sheets like I asked?"
With Susannah, you stand at least a fifty-fifty chance of de-
flecting her if you abruptly change the subject.

"Yes, I washed them. And that's another thing, I don't see
why that had to be my job."

"You do want clean bedding for tonight, don't you?"

Susannah stomped her right foot and slapped the kitchen
table so hard it must have jarred poor Shnookums. At any
rate, he yelped. "Oh no, I'm not, Magdalena. I'm not sleeping
up there where somebody just died."

"Then pick a spot on the floor in the parlor," I told her.
"You're for sure not sleeping with me."

"Magdalena!"

I reminded Susannah that Grandma Yoder had died in my
bedroom, in fact in my very bed. That did the trick. Susannah

had always been a little afraid of Grandma Yoder, although I can't say that I blamed her. Grandma Yoder had been a gaunt, hollow-eyed, perpetually angry woman as far back as I can remember. She died when Susannah was only five, but my sister remembers seeing the old woman standing at the foot of her bed on at least two occasions after that. And, as I've already shared with you, I've seen her about myself a number of times. Apparently these were facts Susannah had forgotten.

"Your room, where sweet young Linda expired, is in the new wing. Grandma was never in there," I reminded her. "And besides which, since you'll be by yourself, you can watch TV all night."

Susannah was cooperative after that.

Even by the time I got done with the few supper dishes, without Susannah's help of course, virtually everyone else had retired to their rooms. Or so I thought. I nearly let out a scream when I came back from checking the front door and found Joel Teitlebaum crouching on the floor behind the check-in desk.

"What on earth are you doing?" I asked, when I finally had control of my vocal cords.

Joel stood up sheepishly. He held up a fistful of postcards. "I was looking at these, trying to pick out a couple to buy, when they all kind of just slipped out of my hand."

I took a couple of deep breaths. "Well, you almost scared the life out of me. I thought everyone had gone to their rooms."

Joel tucked most of the postcards back on the rack. "I'm off to bed myself, soon as I pay for these. It's been a long day, even if it is early."

"You were fond of Linda, weren't you?" I wasn't being nosy, just sympathetic in my own way.

"Yeah, Linda was okay," said Joel. That's one thing I like about young people today. They're seldom maudlin.

"I'm sure you'll miss her. I'll bet you two were really close."

Joel cleared his throat before speaking. "Miss Yoder, I'm afraid you've got the wrong guy. It wasn't me and Linda who were close, it was Linda and Billy Dee."

"I see." I should have seen earlier. How uncharacteristically stupid of me. After all, I had seen Billy Dee and Linda having a tête-à-tête over the quilting frame in the dining room, while Joel sat alone in the parlor munching sunflower seeds.

"Good night, Miss Yoder," said Joel. He seemed more embarrassed now than he had a minute ago, when I'd discovered him on his hands and knees.

"Good night, Joel. And thanks for pitching in the other night with your famous broiled bananas. I hear they were the hit of the house. In fact, I was told they were the only thing that appealed to everybody."

Joel blushed. "Yeah, well, I got the recipe from a West African roommate. They're very easy to make. I'm just glad everybody liked them. I felt sorry for Mrs. Ream. Nobody ate her vegetable curry except for we three vegetarians. You'd have thought her own husband would have given it a try."

"I heard it looked pretty bad," I said in Billy Dee's defense.

"Yeah, well, that's still no excuse for being rude."

I refrained from pointing out that Joel probably hadn't

touched Billy Dee's venison stew, or the Congressman's beans, which had been doctored up with bits of bacon. There is no point in trying to change someone else's perspective, anyway. We all just see what we want to see. That goes double for the young. I decided to just ignore his comment.

"Say, Joel," I said, "you wouldn't be interested in playing a game of cards would you?"

He looked at me in surprise.

"Oh, not with face cards," I assured him quickly. "We Mennonites don't use those. I'm thinking of Rook. I could see if Susannah wants to play, and we could use the kitty as the fourth hand."

I was surprisingly un-tired, given the kind of day I'd had. I would have thought that having a second corpse show up in my inn would wear me to a frazzle, send me emotionally and physically escaping into the depths of dark, safe sleep. But not so. Maybe it was because I'd slept so late that morning, or maybe it was because I'm a psychological misfit, but I was still feeling as perky as all get out. Shamefully so. Maybe even high —not that I'm sure I know what that feels like.

Apparently Joel did not share my vim and vigor; either that or he simply had no interest in playing games with someone old enough to be his mother. He said he was feeling un-usually tired and thought he might even be coming down with something.

We said good night again, and having nothing else to do, I went to my room, lay down on my bed, and began to read. I guess I should confess right now that I absolutely adore reading. I'm sure some people think that just because I live a simple life-style, I have a simple mind. If only they knew.

When I was in the third grade my teacher called Mama in

and told her the school had determined that I had an I.Q. of 146 and they were recommending that I be promoted to the fifth grade. Mama refused to even consider such a thing. Having me skip a grade would lead to prideful and arrogant thoughts on my part, Mama told the teacher. I was never to know I was smarter than anyone else in my class. And then, just to make sure she counteracted anything my teacher might be doing on the sly, Mama established her own program of teaching me all the fine points of modesty and humility.

It wasn't until Susannah was in high school, and she found out from her guidance counselor that she had an I.Q. of 142, that the light began to dawn. If Susannah was that smart, I reasoned, so was I. If not smarter. But by then I had lost confidence in myself and had long since put the idea of college behind me. Still, one day in an argument with Mama, the truth had come out. Just between you and me, Mama deserves a couple of extra turns in her grave for what she did.

Anyway, like I said, I love to read. My books have taken me far beyond the limits of my natural world, and I don't think I could survive my life here at the PennDutch Inn without them. Unfortunately, Hernia doesn't have a library, even a tiny one. Old Doc Shafer does, though. When I was a child he used to bring books by the bushel basket for me to read. Mama didn't mind at all, providing she got to sort through them first.

Nowadays, even the library in Somerset offers slim pickings when it comes to books I haven't read. Fortunately old Doc has a niece in Pittsburgh who visits him almost every other week, and she doesn't seem to mind at all making trips to the Carnegie Library for me. Occasionally she even stops at the Mystery Lovers Bookshop in suburban Oakmont and picks up a good whodunnit or two.

I had just started a book by Paul Theroux, my favorite travel writer, when the phone rang. I answered the phone on the seventh ring, but perhaps I should have waited longer. Even then I must have sounded crabby.

"Miss Yoder?" asked a timid voice.

"That depends on who wants to know."

"This is Melvin, Miss Yoder. Melvin Stoltzfus."

"Speak up, Melvin. I can barely hear you."

"Miss Yoder, I just got a call from the coroner, and there's a couple of questions I'd like to ask."

"Ask away, Melvin."

"Did you know that Linda McMahon was pregnant?"

"She never breathed a word to me about it," I said quite honestly.

"Well, she was. Just about to enter her second trimester, as a matter of fact. Which brings me to my second question. Would you have any idea who the father might be?"

"Why, Melvin Stoltzfus, you should be ashamed!" I said with righteous indignation. "This is a Christian establishment, and I don't allow any hanky-panky. And anyway, you just said yourself that she was three months pregnant. If that's the case, it surely didn't happen here. For all I know, Billy Dee Grizzle is the father."

"Why do you say that?"

"Melvin, dear, I was being flippant."

"I'll have to question Mr. Grizzle about that in the morning," said Melvin, quite seriously. "In the meantime, there's something I think you should know."

"Go on, Melvin, I'm listening."

"Both Heather Brown and Linda McMahon were definitely poisoned."

"I said, go on, Melvin. I already suspected that."

"Both women were killed by the same type of poison, but the killer used two different poisons on Linda McMahon."

"Two poisons?"

I thought I heard Melvin take a deep breath. "Yes, two, but only one of the poisons killed her."

"Come again?"

"You see, Miss Yoder, the poison that killed the women was a very fast-acting type of digitalis. It causes respiratory failure within a matter of minutes. Respiratory failure is when—"

"I know, Melvin. Go on."

"Well, Harrisburg plugged their computer into Washington's and came up with the interesting fact that this particular form of digitalis is found only in one species of plant, and that plant is native only to Morocco."

"Morocco?"

"The lower slopes of the Atlas Mountains to be precise. The Arabic name for the plant is *gouza*. It's a very unusual plant in that it produces green flowers. It's these flowers that are the most toxic part of the plant. Although they are more lethal if consumed fresh, when dried and put into tea they also remain deadly."

It sounded like Melvin was reading a pamphlet the C.I.A. had faxed him. Perhaps he was. "And what about the second poison, the one that didn't kill her?"

"Ah, that. That was just common old *Aethusa cynapium*."

"Sounds common enough to me."

"You know, 'fool's parsley.' "

"Fool's parsley! That stuff grows everywhere you don't want it to. I'm forever trying to get it out of the garden."

"Exactly. So that one at least was easy to come by."

"How toxic is it?"

"Well, let's see. It contains something called *cynapine*, and *cicutoxin*."

"Speak English, Melvin."

"It's apparently not nearly as toxic as that Moroccan plant. People have been known to die from it, but sometimes the symptoms don't even show up for as much as three days. Although they could show up in a few hours, depending on how much the person ate and their general state of health."

"I see. What are the symptoms, Melvin?"

"Well, the coroner didn't say too much about that one, since it isn't the one that killed her . . . no, wait, he did say something about the first symptoms being a general tiredness, a gradual weakening of the muscles."

I tried to remain calm. "Melvin, if it takes a while for the poison in fool's parsley to kick in, isn't it possible that others besides Linda might have eaten some? That the poison might be slowly working in some of us right now?"

I thought I heard Melvin scratch his head. "I suppose that's possible, Miss Yoder, but it doesn't make any sense, does it? The killer used two poisons, remember? If any of you had been given the Moroccan poison, you'd be dead as a doornail by now."

"But Melvin," I foolishly persisted, "what if there are two killers? What if the one who used the Moroccan poison only wanted Miss Brown and Linda dead, but the second one wanted to kill more than just the two women? What if there are two independent killers, with two different agendas, Melvin?"

I'm sorry to say this, Mrs. Stoltzfus, but your son laughed just then. "Magdalena! Susannah was right. You do have an active imagination. Two killers in one place at the same time, with different motives? Do you know what the odds are of such a thing happening?"

What did odds have to do with anything? What were the odds of anybody dying in the PennDutch Inn to begin with? I mean, even Mama and Papa didn't die here, and as for Grandma Yoder, she was ninety-seven and should, by rights, have died in a nursing home. What were the odds that Miss Brown would check in, and then "check out" before she even had a chance to check out? So, what did it matter what the odds were, when Susannah walked in and found Linda dead, clutching in her hands a quilt that wasn't even supposed to be in that room to begin with.

"Forget odds!" I practically screamed. "Use your noggin. Why on earth would someone give a person a slow-acting poison if they were going to give them a fast-acting poison later on? And how come Miss Brown got only one poison when Linda got two?"

"I didn't appreciate your comment about my head," Melvin snapped. "And as you are a civilian, Miss Yoder, I don't think we need to carry this conversation any further." He hung up.

"But, Melvin, I think I know who one of your killers is," I said anyway.

Immediately, I tried to call Melvin back, but the line was busy. I called at least six more times in the next ten minutes, but it was always the same.

Finally I gave up and rang old Doc instead. He picked up on the first ring. "Hello?"

"Doc!" But I never got to say any more than that. Because at that very second the door to my bedroom opened and Billy Dee Grizzle stepped in. In his hand he carried the same hunting knife he'd used to skin the buck.

# Chapter Twenty-three

"Put the phone down," he said softly.

I obeyed.

"Now come here."

I got off the bed, where I'd been sitting, and tried to take a step in his direction. But I found that my feet had suddenly been rooted to the floor. I willed them to move, but they would have no part of it.

"I said, get over here."

I opened my mouth to speak, but no words came out.

Billy Dee took a couple of steps forward, the knife plainly in view. "I'm sorry to say this, Miss Yoder, but if you don't cooperate, I'm going to have to slice you wide open like that buck this afternoon." He ran the tip of the knife lightly across his clothing, from his throat down to his groin. "Then I'm going to gut you."

I screamed then, at least in my mind, but no sound came

out that I could hear. Like Susannah, I had become a silent screamer.

Billy Dee sprang forward and grabbed me by the hair with his left hand. Then he spun me around and slipped his right arm around my neck. The tip of the knife now rested against that soft spot between the back of my left ear and my skull. "Walk!"

I commanded my feet to walk. Like reluctant and disorganized troops, my feet at last obeyed, and I lurched forward. With each step, I could feel the tip of the knife prick into my skin. With each breath I took, I could smell Billy Dee's breath, which was saturated with alcohol. Like a monstrous pair of mating beetles, we staggered in tandem to the door.

"The kitchen," he grunted.

Maybe it was Billy Dee's breath, or maybe simply because my mind was no longer able to sustain such heights of terror, but I felt a sort of awakening. A tap had been turned back on, and energy that had been temporarily dammed up was flowing back through me. I no longer had to command each foot to move, remember to take each breath.

As soon as the kitchen door closed behind us, Billy Dee let go of my hair. With his left hand, he pushed me toward the center of the room.

"Now turn around," he ordered.

I turned.

"Don't even think of running, Miss Yoder. I can hit a stump at fifty yards with this thing."

I just looked at him.

He seemed almost embarrassed. "You know, I kinda liked

you, Miss Yoder. It's a pity you had to go and get yourself involved."

I thought of one or two smart things to say, but bit my tongue.

"Course, now that you are involved, I ain't left with any choice, am I?"

I tried to look motherly, but apparently Billy Dee was beyond guilt. "And it was such a damn good plan, too, Miss Yoder. Letting Jeanette feel just what it's like losing a daughter. Much better than killing her, herself, don't you think?"

Thankfully, after what seemed like an interminable pause, even Billy Dee decided it must have been a rhetorical question. "I didn't mean to kill my only kid," he said quietly. "I sure as hell didn't deserve to go to jail for it. And I sure as hell ain't going again.

"You know, I ain't much of a thinker, but this was one hell of a thought-out plan. Ever since that bitch told me six weeks ago that we was coming down here to protest the Congressman, I knew I had me my chance. We can't afford to let chances pass us up, now can we, Miss Yoder?"

I shook my head. Anything to encourage him to keep on talking. His knife was a lot sharper than his tongue.

"And I've been doing my homework the whole time, too. When I found out that the Congressman had taken him a trip to Morocco, I knew just what I was going to do. You see, they have this wildflower there. Kind of a strange-looking green thing they call—oh, what the hell, I can't remember the name of that damn thing. Some damn Arab word like—"

"*Gouza,*" I said.

"Yeah, that's right." He seemed almost to welcome my

interruption. "Anyway, I got me a buddy, still in the merchant marines, who puts into Tangiers every now and then. He owed me a favor. A big one. And he's got connections, the kind you wouldn't know anything about. So I had him send me some of the stuff. Of course it ain't as potent when it's been dried, but as you can see," he chuckled morbidly, "it's still strong enough to do the job."

"It sounds like you went to an awful lot of trouble," I said. I tried to sound admiring, not critical.

Billy stared at me.

"I mean," I hurried to explain, "there are probably a whole lot of poisons you could have gotten closer to home. Without sending off to Morocco."

He burst out laughing. "But don't you see? That's what I mean about it being one hell of an idea. I knew Jeanette and the Congressman had it in for each other. No siree Bob, that was no secret. Not on Jeanette's part, anyway. She was always making out how she'd been wronged by him. Called him a sleaze. Right in front of Linda." He tapped his forehead with a finger. "Didn't take no genius to figure out that she had been blackmailing him neither."

"Blackmail?"

"Yes, ma'am. Even poor Linda knew about it, and she hated her old mama."

"Linda told you that?"

"A little sweet-talking goes a long way, if you know what I mean."

I wanted to slap the smirk off his face. "That's absolutely disgusting, Billy Dee. Linda was just a child."

"Anyway, once I knew the Congressman was being blackmailed, I knew I had me the perfect scapegoat. What with his drug habit and all, he couldn't afford no blackmail. Coming up with the Moroccan thing was the easy part."

"You knew about the Congressman's drug abuse too?"

"Like I said, Miss Yoder, I did my homework. Then I made sure that another interested party knew just as much as I did. Kinda gave her a motive to match her husband's."

"Not Lydia!"

"Hell, yes. And that's a damn shame too. Pretty woman like that shouldn't have to hear such things."

"But why would Lydia go after Linda? You'd think it would be Jeanette or Garrett she'd want to punish."

"And what better way to punish them both, Miss Yoder?"

"But what about the baby, Billy Dee? You knew Linda was pregnant, didn't you? How could you kill your own baby? Especially after having lost Jennifer Mae?"

For a few seconds Billy Dee's upper lip quivered. "Leave Jennifer Mae out of this, Miss Yoder! I didn't know Linda was pregnant until just a week or so ago. By then it was too late, of course."

"How was it too late?"

"The wheels of justice had already begun to turn, Miss Yoder." He laughed. "You see, justice must be served, Miss Yoder, at all costs."

"Even at the cost of your own flesh and blood?"

Billy Dee responded by plunging the knife into my kitchen table. The blade seemed to penetrate about an inch into the hard, aged wood. For a split second I considered bolting for the door, but in that split second Billy Dee pulled the blade out again. It gleamed, just as wicked and sharp-looking as ever.

"Any more questions, Miss Yoder?"

I swallowed the cantaloupe in my throat. My prognosis did not look very good. If I was going to check out, I might as well go with all my questions answered. "Yes, actually, I do have another question. What did Miss Brown have to do with all this? Why did you kill her? You did kill her, didn't you, Billy Dee?"

A big smile crept across his face, the kind of smile that signals smug satisfaction. "Ah, Miss Brown. Yeah, I killed Miss Brown, or whatever her name was. Only it sure as hell wasn't Brown. That bitch was a Fed."

"What is a Fed?" Look, there isn't any point in worrying about appearing stupid when you are about to die.

Billy Dee's smile softened and appeared almost benevolent. Perhaps the man had a knack for teaching, particularly slow learners. "A Fed is a Federal Drug Enforcement Officer. Miss Brown, or whoever the hell she was, was one busy woman. She had a line on my buddy's connections back in Morocco. One of them was an American who liked to ship stuff back home." His smile slipped into a laugh. "It's a small world, ain't it, Miss Yoder?"

"I don't know. I've seen too little of it to tell."

"Then that's a shame," said Billy, and it sounded like he really meant it. "But take my word for it, it's a real small world. Real small. Turns out Miss Brown, or whoever, also had a line on the Congressman. And guess what? Them two lines was tangled. Seems that good old Garrett was buying from my Moroccan supplier on a regular basis. Not too dumb a move on his part, either, because them South American sources are too closely watched these days.

"Anyway, this woman comes here to see if she can catch the Congressman with his fingers in the sugar bowl, *before* he can check into that clinic—uh—"

"Grossinger-Beechman."

"Yeah, that's the place. Y'see, if she coulda done that, she'da had leverage. Might have been able to pull in a whole handful of lines; most of them with one end tied to Morocco."

"And one of them yours?"

He looked surprised, and then amused. "Hell, no! I don't do drugs."

"You just buy deadly poison?"

"Yeah, you might say that. Real deadly poison. The best. Anyway, I wasn't afraid that Miss Brown would arrest me— it'd take a lot more than her to put me in the slammer again. What I didn't want, though, was her ruining it all by reeling in the Congressman before I had a chance to pin Linda's death on him. So, I took me a vote and decided that Miss Brown would take a nice trip down them stairs, after she had a taste of *gouza*."

"I'm sure you'd make a good cruise director, but I'm also sure Miss Brown didn't swallow your *gouza* willingly."

He laughed surprisingly loud. Surely someone had heard him. "She was a feisty little woman, for her age, I'll give her that. Course, I set me up a diversion, just in case there was any noise, by putting that spider on Linda's bed. Anybody who knew Linda, knew how she felt about bugs, specially spiders. And finding one here was a piece of cake. Face it, Miss Yoder, you ain't much of a housekeeper."

Even while sitting in the lap of death, I felt my face sting at such an accusation. "It was Susannah's room!"

His eyes twinkled cruelly. "This one I found in the dining room, on one of them corncobs you got there. Stuck him in that jar you let me have for them night crawlers. Honestly, Miss Yoder, I don't mean no disrespect, but a farm woman like you oughta know don't nobody go fishing in November with worms."

"But Papa . . ." Then I remembered that February was the off-season month Papa fished in, only it was ice-fishing, and he used smoked bacon for bait.

"Yes siree Bob! This here spider was a nice, plump little critter. And I wouldn't have had no place to keep him if it hadn't been for that jar you so kindly gave me."

"That jar! I—uh—I saw it in Miss Brown's room."

"Did you now? Well, it ain't there no more. Didn't get me a chance to go back that night to get it. Woulda been too noisy with that room sealed up like it is. But I finally got it. Of course I shoulda figured a snoop like you, with all the time in the world, would beat me in there."

"I am not a snoop," I said. If I was going to die, I at least wanted to set the record straight.

"And I suppose you figured out it was me who broke into the old bag's trunk?"

"Not soon enough, I'm afraid."

"Of course there weren't nothing in there to worry about. What a waste of time and energy. No papers or nothing mentioning me or the Congressman. 'Tweren't nothing at all in there, as you know."

"Except for a sunflower seed. You should be ashamed of yourself for trying to pin everything on a nice young kid like Joel."

Billy Dee shrugged. "Somebody's gotta take the rap, and it

sure as hell ain't gonna be me. But how did you know it wasn't Teitlebaum who opened the trunk?"

"You left your calling card at the scene of the crime. Tobacco kills, you know."

"So do knives," said Billy Dee softly. It took only a glance at the knife to drive the point home.

I tried to think of a stalling device. "I could fix you a cup of coffee, if you want. And a bacon and tomato sandwich. It won't take any time at all."

Billy Dee pulled a small vial of pale emerald-colored liquid out of his shirt pocket.

"Speaking of time, Miss Yoder. Just a few drops of this stuff on the tongue, and you're a goner. Of course, Miss Brown didn't open her mouth voluntarily, but it weren't really no harder than giving a cat or dog a pill. You ever done that, Miss Yoder? Given an animal a pill?"

"Some cats scratch pretty bad," I said. "They also make a lot of noise when they die. Why don't you just take off, Billy Dee? You got what you came for. Why don't you just cut the phone cords, let all the air out of our tires, and take off? It's six miles into town, and you could be halfway to Maryland before I got that far."

In response, Billy Dee yanked the knife out of the table and began scraping at the stubble on his cheeks. The blade was obviously razor sharp; little bits of whisker fell like pepper from a mill.

I could think of nothing further to say.

"Well, now, Miss Yoder," said Billy Dee, filling in the silence, "we've done far too much talking tonight. It's time for a little action, don't you think?"

"I don't know what you mean," I struggled to say.

"Sure, you do. You're a fine-looking woman. A whole lot prettier than that Miss Brown. It's time you and me had a little fun before we have to say good-bye."

I knew that if I didn't sit down then, I would probably faint. I tried to speak, but what came out wasn't words.

"What was that?"

"Please, Billy, may I sit down?" I managed to say.

"Sit." He kicked a chair under me and slowly moved the knife back up to my throat. With his free hand, he began to stroke my hair. "When you catch your breath, Miss Yoder, you and me are going for a little walk."

I tried to catch my breath, but it seemed like I had rocks in my lungs. "Where are we going, Billy?"

His hand left my hair and slid to my face. "I seen you looking at me when we was in the barn, Miss Yoder. It was you put the idea in my head. That's a mighty fine barn, Miss Yoder, so I figure you and me are going to put it to good use."

"But Mose will be there," I said. "One of the cows is ill, and he likes to stay the night when that happens." It was of course a lie, but one of which even Mama would have been proud.

"I ain't afraid of no old man," said Billy. He sounded almost happy at the thought of a confrontation with Mose. "Now, it's about time we head on out for there. I got me a lot to do yet before the night is over."

"I can't move with this knife at my throat," I said.

He pulled the knife back a few inches to allow me room to stand. "Now, get up."

"Billy, please," I begged. "You can tie me up here if you

want to. Gag me, even. And then take off. I won't cause any trouble until morning."

I thought I heard Billy Dee grunt in anger then. I closed my eyes and waited for the slicing edge of the knife, or at the least to feel the onslaught of his fists. I would rather have died with Mama and Papa in the tunnel, but if this was how I had to go, I prayed he would do it quickly.

But no pain was forthcoming. Instead, the knife seemed to drop into my lap, and then slid harmlessly to the floor. I heard the ping of its blade as it struck the linoleum. As for Billy Dee, by the sound of it, he too had hit the floor, just seconds after the knife.

I kept my eyes closed, afraid that if I opened them the horror would somehow return.

I felt a hand on my shoulder, not Billy's, that much I knew. "Magdalena?"

I forced my eyes open and could hardly believe what I saw. "Doc!" I screamed.

The hand on my shoulder patted me gently.

"There, there, Magdalena, it's all right now. The son of a bitch is out like a prizefighter. Of course I gave him twice the dose I gave Susannah."

"What?"

Old Doc waved the syringe proudly. "I'm just glad the bastard didn't hear me sneaking in and turn around. Anyway, what's good for the goose is good for the gander, like they say. When you hung up on me, I knew something was terribly wrong. Would have gotten here even sooner, but I had to wait two minutes until it was time for my damn cake to come out of the oven. Of course I didn't get a chance to frost it."

"What?"

Doc smiled magnanimously. "No big deal. It'll be nice and cool by the time I get back. Best time to frost it anyway. Shall I make it chocolate or vanilla? Which do you prefer?"

"Caramel," I said, just to be difficult.

# Chapter Twenty-four

By tacit agreement, we waited until our second piece of cake before we brought up the previous night's events and the circumstances leading up to them. The first piece of cake, both Doc and I understood instinctively, was to be savored. One can't pay proper attention to aroma, texture, and taste when one is talking.

Having swallowed my first bite of the second piece, I felt free to fill Doc in on some of the missing pieces of the story.

"It was the quilt," I said. "That was the main thing. It kept bothering me in the back of my mind, but I was just too stupid to see it. I should have known right away, of course, when I saw Linda clutching Mama's Dresden Plate quilt."

It is permissible to talk with cake in your mouth, if you're on your second piece, so Doc did. "What's so damn special about that quilt? As I recall, you keep quilts in all the rooms."

"But that's it exactly! Every room has a quilt in it, but it's a particular quilt. Each room has a quilt with a different pattern on it. This quilt, the Dresden Plate quilt that Mama made, belongs in Billy Dee's room, not Linda's!

"So you see, when I saw it in Linda's room, I knew something was out of place, but it just didn't register."

"Couldn't Mr. Grizzle simply have loaned it to Linda?"

I shoved in a bite of Doc's incredibly moist cake. "As a matter of fact, that's exactly what happened. Linda had mentioned to Billy Dee that she was feeling chilly, and so he offered to bring her a cup of herbal tea and an extra quilt. Of course, that was the perfect opportunity for Billy Dee to administer the poison.

"As soon as the poison started to take effect, Billy Dee grabbed the teacup and extra quilt and got out of there."

"I see," said Doc, "except that Mr. Grizzle, being your average, insensitive man, grabbed the wrong quilt."

"Well, they do look sort of alike," I surprised myself by saying in Billy Dee's defense. "Linda's original quilt was also a Dresden Plate pattern, but it wasn't the one Mama made." I swallowed hard and let the truth out. "Mama's quilt isn't nearly so nice." Sorry, Mama, about that extra spin.

"More coffee, Magdalena?"

I nodded. "The weird part is, Doc, that Billy Dee seemed like such a nice man. He was always so polite to me, of course until last night."

"Never fully trust anyone, Magdalena," said old Doc sagely. "Want some more cake?"

I shook my head. "But Lydia, that was even more of a surprise."

"Do tell," Doc urged. "Melvin was rather cryptic when I called him this morning. Seems he's not happy about having to share credit with you."

"Ah, forget Melvin. He's going out with Susannah tonight anyway. That's payback enough.

"But back to Lydia. She too made a complete confession last night. I hate to say it, but Billy Dee was right on the money. Well, sort of. It was she who took the potshots at me. She'd stayed home that morning while Delbert attempted to take Garrett to the clinic. Apparently the Reams had had a fight that morning, because Garrett refused to clear some things up before his admission. Garrett, I mean the Congressman, changed his mind on the way there, but that's another story.

"Anyway, when Lydia saw me set out for Freni's across the field, she assumed it was Jeanette, possibly even meeting Garrett on a secret rendezvous. When she figured out it was me in the woods, she backed off. It was on her way back to the house, out by the barn, that she walked through some fool's parsley, and the idea of poisoning Jeanette popped into her head.

"Although Lydia's main objective was to get even with Jeanette, and to clear her out of the way for her husband's presidential bid, she was not particularly reluctant to poison poor Linda as well. After all, Linda was concrete proof of her husband's infidelity. Lydia, of course, knew that her husband wouldn't eat that dreadful curry. He hates garlic, and she put four whole cloves in it."

Doc hadn't gotten a chance to appreciate any of Lydia's finer qualities. "Yeah," he said, "but she sure as hell didn't care if she poisoned the rest of you. That woman deserves to fry until she's a nice golden brown."

I chuckled, perhaps inappropriately. "Whatever her ulti-mate punishment is, Doc, she's suffering plenty in the meantime. Worst case of flea bites I've ever seen. It was like those fleas were just waiting for a nice, cultured English woman to come along and be their dinner."

Doc smiled with satisfaction. "What about the Congressman's aide, Mr. James, isn't it? At dinner the other night you intimated that he and Mrs. Ream might be sweet on each other."

I held out my cup for more coffee. "So I was wrong, Doc. That was all an act, at least on her part, to exercise control over him. Delbert, on the other hand, might well have a thing for Lydia. Melvin thinks it might have been Delbert shooting at Jeanette that first day out in the woods. He does, after all, carry a revolver to protect the Congressman."

Doc put down the coffeepot. "Or, it simply might have been the Congressman who shot at Jeanette, using his aide's revolver. Unfortunately, we'll probably never know the whole truth. Both of those men are as slippery as three-day-old meat."

I was glad it was just cake we were eating and not a main meal. "At any rate, Doc, I think it's possible that Delbert does carry a torch for Lydia. He was pretty broken up when Melvin arrested her. Anyway, he seemed much too eager to come across as gay, if you ask me."

"Like he was sending up a smoke screen?"

"Exactly. But Lydia actually despises the man. Seems she blames him for keeping her husband supplied with drugs, and for keeping the secret of his affair with Jeanette for so long. By her own admission, she would have been happy to have him chow down on her vegetable curry as well, but she forgot that he's allergic to garlic and therefore wouldn't touch the stuff, even though he likes the taste.

"Unfortunately, poor Joel, who isn't even on her hate list, had to suffer. But he's doing all right now in the hospital. Jeanette's still in critical condition, but I'm pretty sure she'll pull through. After all, only the good die young."

"Which means you were safe all along," Doc teased.

I felt a goose walk over my grave.

"Maybe. But you know, I would have eaten Lydia's vegetable curry if I had been there."

Suddenly I felt angry, both at Lydia, who had violated my trust, and at Freni, whose fragile ego had given rise to the whole situation to begin with.

"One thing's for certain, Doc, I'm never letting any guests in my kitchen ever again. Not even if I have to cook every meal myself."

"Good idea," Doc agreed. "There should never be more than one cook at a time in a kitchen. Two maybe, at the very most. Like they say, too many cooks spoil the broth."

"Make that crooks, Doc."

We both laughed, and I poured some more coffee. "Say, Doc, I might just be going on a date this weekend," I said shyly.

Doc beamed. "I haven't asked you yet, but sure thing, kid."

I patted his free hand warmly. "Thanks, Doc, but it's with someone else."

Doc's face clouded over. "Sam didn't leave his wife, did he?"

"Get real, Doc. Jumbo Jim called me this morning. We talked for almost an hour."

"You mean that hot dog fella down in Baltimore?"

"Chicken, Doc. And that's the one. Turns out he got my

number from information. He wants to come up this weekend and meet me. He thinks we might have a lot in common."

"Why? Is he rich?"

I tried to look aghast but found myself giggling instead. "I don't know if he's rich, Doc. But we both run small businesses, and he's my age—"

"Ah, so that's it! You don't have time for an old, bald man. Think I've lost the spark, eh?"

"Grass doesn't grow on a busy street, Doc," I said quickly. I had no idea what that meant, but I'd heard Susannah say it once or twice when she had bald boyfriends.

"And there's no snow on the roof when there's a fire inside," added Doc. He seemed to have perked up.

"Like I said, Doc, this is only a maybe. He might not even show up."

"Here's hoping he doesn't," said Doc, as he served me up another slice of his deliciously moist cake.

I ate it anyway.

# Chapter Twenty-five

## DOC SHAFER'S COCOA MOCHA CAKE

   2 cups sifted flour
1 ½ cups sugar
   4 tablespoons cocoa powder
   1 tablespoon instant coffee powder
   1 teaspoon baking powder
   1 teaspoon baking soda
   ½ teaspoon salt
   ¾ cup softened butter
   2 eggs
   1 cup milk

Mix the dry ingredients together in a large bowl. Add butter and eggs. Stir. Add milk and beat well until the batter is smooth. Pour the batter into two 8-inch layer pans that have been greased and floured. Bake at 350 degrees for 40 minutes, or until a toothpick inserted in the center of the cakes comes out clean. Ice when cool.

## DOC'S CARAMEL ICING

2 cups brown sugar
1 cup heavy cream
3 tablespoons butter
$\frac{1}{2}$ teaspoon vanilla
Pinch of salt

Cook the sugar and cream over low heat for about a half hour. The cooking is done when a sample of the mixture forms a soft ball when dropped into cold water. At that point, remove the pot from the heat and stir in the butter, vanilla, and salt. Continue to stir until the mixture reaches spreading consistency.